RACHAEL'S
POINT

RACHAEL'S POINT

R. I. KING

iUniverse

RACHAEL'S POINT

This is a work of fiction. All of the characters, names, incidents, organizations, and dialogue in this novel are either the products of the author's imagination or are used fictitiously.

iUniverse books may be ordered through booksellers or by contacting:

iUniverse
1663 Liberty Drive
Bloomington, IN 47403
www.iuniverse.com
1-800-Authors (1-800-288-4677)

ISBN: 978-1-5320-2453-5 (sc)
ISBN: 978-1-5320-2454-2 (hc)
ISBN: 978-1-5320-2455-9 (e)

Library of Congress Control Number: 2017909915

Print information available on the last page.

iUniverse rev. date: 06/24/2017

Chapter 1

Rod Strickland settled into his window seat on the 747 that would take him to his hometown, and he watched the other passengers as they boarded and passed him in the aisle. As usual, he was in the second aisle, a window seat in first class, on the pilot's side of the plane. This was not a superstition; it was a strategy. He liked to see the looks on passengers' faces as they turned the corner with their carry-on luggage. The businessman whose expression showed anxiety, wanting to get to his seat and look at reports and reviews. The mother with the two children about five and seven years old. The older boy saying, "Is this our seat?" as he passed each row. The younger boy holding his mother's hand and taking in the wonders of the seats and overhead bins; this was obviously his first flight.

Rod would look at all of the passengers and make a mental note. He could not help himself; it was instinctive. He did the same with the crew. This crew was made up of six attendants, four female and two males, all under the age of thirty. They looked fit, wore smiles, and could have done a commercial for the airlines on looks alone. With everyone boarded, he looked out the window and saw the baggage being loaded onto the plane by three burly men who had no expressions on their faces.

With his observation being completed, like clockwork, the first-class attendant, Olivia, asked him, "What would you like to drink?" He chose tea with lemon. When Olivia brought him the tea, he took a sip and began thinking of how, when he'd left his hometown, he'd sworn that he would never return. It had been twenty-four years since he had been at Rachael's Point. Twenty-four years since he'd been forced to join the military, where he'd learned to fight and kill with the black-ops team.

Twenty-four years over which he had completed over thirty missions, killing the enemies of the United States government. It had been four years of honing his skill to kill. These events eventually led him to the conclusion that God did not exist.

One particular incident stuck out in his mind. He and his team were assigned to take out one of the cleric's generals who was suspected of financing suicide bombers in the region. Government intelligence had pinpointed the general's location. Rod had entered the home with ease, and with one skilled move, Cleric Musaad's neck was broken as he sat in his chair watching a report of the latest bombing of a fruit market that had killed forty-three people. Rod had no remorse in killing Musaad, not even as he turned to leave and came face-to-face with the dead man's wife and two daughters, who had suddenly appeared in the room. With still no regrets, there were three shots, three deaths. If there was a God, Rod surely would die before this day was over. Rod did not die, but he received the Distinguished Service Cross from his government. No God, no Buddha, no nothing had punished him for those or any other deaths. He decided that if he could kill with no repercussions, then there was no supreme being that sat on high.

Rod Strickland was the only son of David and Nancy Strickland, a gardener and a teacher, respectively. Both had died tragically in an automobile accident when Rod was fourteen. Though many knew him, they did not know how he would survive in the foster care program. Rod was not a troublemaker; as a matter of fact, he was nondescript. He was an average student in school and didn't play any sports, but if prompted for conversation, he would make people feel like he was interested in what they were saying. He was respectful, and it appeared that he was a follower. He seemed most comfortable when he was with his three friends: Donald O'Connor Jr., Don Hart, and his best friend Ronnie Parker. It came to no one's surprise that Mrs. Parker took Rod into her home after the death of his parents. With the help of the district attorney's office, this was satisfactory to the Department of Children Services.

Rod never had a strong religious background. While he grew up, his parents would say, "We are CME churchgoers. We go on Christmas, Mother's Day, and Easter." Rod didn't think about God one way or another until his parents died. He had a brief thought at the gravesite that if there was a God, his parents were with him; if not, then his parents were simply dead. His goal now was to graduate from high school, go to a state teacher's college (his mother's directive), and then teach high school until he was ready to retire.

The years he lived with the Parkers helped him realize that it was all right to be a teenager and have fun. There were game nights, breakfast for dinner, and even family movie night. He never looked at Mrs. Parker as a mother, but as an aunt. Because neither of Rod's parents had any siblings, he had no aunts or uncles, and his grandparents had died before he was born. He was a relatively happy teenager in the Parker household. That was when the bond between Ronnie and him grew the most.

Things changed when he was forced to go into the military. By the time he had finished with basic training, that relatively happy teenager had become an internally bitter and angry young man. He was top in the self-defense, marksmanship, and strategic planning courses. This did not go unnoticed by those in charge. Prior to graduation from basic training, he was offered an opportunity to train and be assigned to an elite branch of the army. Rod accepted without hesitation and excelled in the new training. He became an expert in decisive action, stealth combat, weaponry, and acts of violence, which he termed acts of killing.

Devoid of all ethics with regard to the enemy, Rod completed his eighteen-month training and was assigned to the CIA along with five other operatives. They had not trained together but had similar backgrounds. Their parents were deceased due to an accident, they were assigned straight from basic training, they were at the top of their classes, and none of them believed in God.

But five years ago, Rod changed his mind. He had an encounter with God that caused him to realize that not only was there a God, but God was involved in the lives of all his children. It occurred as he was on his way home from work as a consultant and research analyst for the government. His job was to speak with groups of young men and women at colleges and universities. He would tell them about the benefits of government service, and on occasion he could identify a student for the black-ops program. On that day, he was waiting in traffic behind a school bus that had stopped to let off some children. Out of the corner of his eye, he saw a semitrailer truck going too fast to stop at the intersection. Suddenly, a woman wearing a black duster appeared out of nowhere and was running alongside the truck's trailer. When she caught up to the cabin, she jumped onto the step of the truck, her black duster flapping in the wind. She had moved with the grace of a jungle cat, and her short brown hair blew in the wind. When she leaped, the form-fitting black pants that she wore revealed the taut muscles in her calves and thighs that had catapulted her onto the step of the truck. This lady, this angel, was on the step of the semi, turning the wheel and straightening the fishtailing trailer, stopping the truck fifty feet away from the bus and unsuspecting children.

Unusual as this was, it was not what brought on Rod's epiphany. It was the fact that no one else had seen the black clad angel. When the police arrived, the driver of the semi was still unconscious; he was taken in an ambulance with a heart attack. The police asked what had happened, and understandably neither the kids nor the bus driver could tell them. After identifying himself, Rod volunteered to the police what he saw. The obvious questions followed. Where was the lady, and where did she go after performing this miraculous feat that no one else could verify? What did she look like? All he could remember was that fluttering black duster and the athleticism and grace with which she moved.

The official newspaper report said that the driver, before passing out, was able to bring the semi to a stop. From that day, Rod realized that there had been divine intervention in that incident. Not just a higher being, but a creator who cared, and who was aware of the past, present, and future. One who would "encamp angels around you," as he had heard more than one television preacher say when he stopped to listen on occasion, mocking their suits or their speech. This incident put Rod on a path to study the Judeo-Christian God, his son, and the angels that attended to both God and man. Over the last five years, Rod had been sharing his beliefs and studies with others. Today he was considered one of the top twenty experts in the country on the subject of angels. He was on his way back to Rachael's Point and, beknownst to him, another encounter with the lady in the black duster.

CHAPTER 2

R od landed at the small Rachael's Point airport, where he was met by his best friend from high school and the main reason he'd accepted the speaking engagement back in his hometown.

Ronnie Parker smiled as he hugged his friend. "Great seeing you. You look great."

"So do you, Ronnie."

As they grabbed Rod's carry-on bags, Rod felt as if he were being watched. When he turned, he could have sworn he saw a woman in a black duster turning the corner and heading toward the baggage claim area. The inside of the airport was not large. Once he stepped through the doors from the runway where he'd departed the plane, there were chairs for those who were awaiting the arrival of their departing flights. One hundred feet behind them on the left was the area where people waiting to meet the arriving passengers were allowed to stand. On the right, also one hundred feet behind the chairs, was the security check-in. Behind those areas were the lobby, the ticket counters, and the baggage claim. That was where Rod thought he saw the woman turn the corner, behind those who were waiting for friends and loved ones to arrive.

As he looked around, he noticed there were a lot of people in long, black trench coats. This was what people wore in Pennsylvania in late October. The temperature was thirty-four degrees according to the pilot, and the winds were high. As he got into the 1966 GTO that Ronnie had received as a high school graduation present, the lady in the duster went out of his mind.

"Well," Ronnie said, "you are scheduled to speak Saturday night at 8:00 p.m."

"I thought it was going to be Sunday morning."

Ronnie laughed. "That was all changed by the committee of one, Commissioner Hart."

"Hart?" Rod echoed.

"Yes. He's been the city manager since the death of Carter."

Don Hart had wanted to be city manager since they were in high school. He was the only high school student in their class who attended city council meetings with prepared questions. Donnie, as the group of the Four called him, was a nerd, but he knew how to spin issues so that they would benefit him. This had finally paid off. He was Commissioner Carter's biggest fan in public, but behind the scenes, he worked to block every issue or program that Carter tried to bring to the city. This was no different than when they were in high school: Don had encouraged Carter to go after the girl and then disparaged him when his back was turned.

"How did Carter die?" Rod asked.

"He was murdered in the driveway of his home. No suspects, no apparent motive, just a random act."

"Who is investigating the murder?"

"Dobie," answered Ronnie.

"Dobie!"

"He's the lead detective on the case."

"Dobie?" Rod repeated, even more surprised. *Donald J. O'Connor Jr.,* thought Rod. *Star high school athlete, winner of the most valuable player award, winner of the Cambria's County's Mr. Basketball award, and recipient of a full football and basketball scholarship to Ohio State University, Harvard University, and Edinboro State College.* Donald J. O'Connor Jr., the son of District Attorney Donald J. O'Connor Sr. Junior, as Senior called him, would rather be known as Dobie, a name he received from his tenth-grade football coach, Mr. Danshac. No one knew what Dobie meant, but the name stuck, much to the displeasure of Donald Sr.

Dobie had turned down all three college offers. Instead, he went to the state police academy, where he came out at the bottom of his class. He would have been thrown out for failing to control his anger with other cadets had it not been for his father's connections. Upon graduation,

Dobie joined the Rachael's Point Police Department as a patrolman. Many believed that because he was the son of the district attorney, he became a detective before he was qualified. Dobie was the fourth member of Rod and Ronnie's high school clique. He was smart, but he was much better at being an intimidator. In high school, he'd been six foot two and weighed two hundred pounds. He was not too fat, but solid. Back then, he had played tight end and defensive end on the football team, and he was the center on the basketball team. Dobie O'Connor was the enforcer; if he told the group they were going to do something, they did it—not out of fear, but out of self-preservation. At least, that was how they saw it back in high school. That was part of the reason Rod had joined the army and was later was assigned to the black-ops. Dobie had said that Rod would always be a punk and would never be able to defend himself or anyone else. The black-ops program soon changed this assessment, as well as many of Rod's other perceptions.

Ronnie watched as Rod clenched his teeth. "Let it go," he offered, breaking into his friend's thoughts.

"Let it go!" Rod parroted sarcastically as they were pulling up to Ronnie's parents' house.

"Man, it was twenty-four years ago. This coming Saturday is the exact anniversary date."

Rod did not need to be reminded. He was the one banished from Rachael's Point. He was the one everyone had thought—and probably still thought—got away with murder.

Rod said, "Doesn't this bring back memories? How many times have we pulled into this driveway together, on the verge of an argument, and the smell of food coming from the house caused us to stop and concentrate on who was going to get to the table first?"

"It does bring back good memories, doesn't it?" Ronnie agreed.

"Ronnie, I did not even ask. How is your mom?"

"Oh, wow! You don't know. She died eight years ago. I tried to contact you through the government and through your agency, but you were on a tour in Michigan, and then you went on to Montreal."

"That's no excuse." Rod clenched his teeth and felt an increase in his heart rate. He was now angry. "You had no problem tracking me down for this speaking engagement."

"Yeah, but you were at your house in Dallas."

"What happened? How did she die?"

"Natural causes," Ronnie said a little too fast and with little emotion.

"Natural causes? Did you ask for an autopsy?"

"Dobie did not think it was necessary," Ronnie explained.

"Dobie! But what does *he* have to do with any of this?"

Ronnie did not want to be pressed further. "Rod, let it go," he said before taking a bag from Rod and heading upstairs.

"Rod, let it go!" Rod had heard that statement before now, and before Ronnie's outburst earlier in the car. They'd been seventeen, and all four of them had been at the junior/ senior prom. Dobie, who was being his usual arrogant self, had just interrupted Rod's dance with Wanda Hall. It had taken Rod two months to get up the nerve to ask her to the prom, and he'd spent another two months learning how to dance. Now that he had her in his arms, Dobie interrupted him to talk about their plan (or rather, Dobie's plan) for after the prom. Rod shoved Dobie and yelled, "Are you nuts?" Rod remembered yelling at Dobie and shoving him, much to the disgust of Wanda. She then walked away from the two of them.

Dobie had glared at her. "See?" he taunted Rod. "She really didn't want to dance."

Incensed at his friend's deliberate provocation, Rod charged at Dobie and would have put a serious hurting on him were it not for Ronnie pulling him back and telling him to let it go.

Dobie had a look of triumph on his face, and he put his arm around Rod's shoulder and told him, "Here is the plan."

Let it go, Rod thought again as he was walking upstairs behind Ronnie. But that was easier said than done. There would be no letting it go, because nothing that involved Dobie was ever that simple. Mrs. Parker, the lady who'd taken him in after his parents had died, had supposedly died of natural causes. Something wasn't right. He owed it to her to find out the real cause of her death. He would make some calls to his associates, and they would do the rest.

As Rod began to unpack, the phone rang, and Ronnie left the room to answer it. Rod walked over to the window of his old room and looked out on Menoher Boulevard. He froze. Standing across the street and wearing a black duster with a white button-down shirt, black jeans, and black boots was his short, brown-haired angel, the elusive figure who had changed his life. Not wanting to lose her again, Rod furiously tapped on the window. When she looked up, he signaled to her that he was coming down, and for her not to go. As he started down the stairs, he heard Ronnie on the phone saying, "Don't worry, I won't screw up. He is here, and he will be there on time. I know everything depends on the proper timing."

When Ronnie turned and saw him in the doorway, Rod thought there was a look of fear—or maybe it was surprise—on his friend's face. But Rod couldn't stop now to speculate. He needed to get to the duster lady, and fast. As he rushed out the door, he barely heard Ronnie frantically calling after him.

Rod looked up and down the street. He was too late; the duster lady had vanished. "God, where did she go?" he said to himself. She was gone, but how could that be?

Back inside the house, Ronnie was ending his conversation when Rod returned. "Everything all right?" Ronnie asked.

"Yes. I want to go visit the gravesite and pay my respects to your mother, and to Darlene."

"Really?" Ronnie said calmly.

Rod looked at him with a smile. "Let it go. I will be ready after I take a shower."

"Okay," Ronnie said. "I just need to go out for fifteen or twenty minutes."

"Sure," Rod said as he climbed the stairs.

As he stepped into the shower, Rod thought about Mrs. Parker fixing breakfast for him and Ronnie. The two boys became friends in fourth grade and were quickly inseparable. They were roommates when the sixth-grade class went on a field trip to Washington, DC. In the seventh grade, they scheduled all their classes together and convinced each other to try out for football. Ronnie was the only one who knew that Rod was in love with Wanda Hall. Though he tried to persuade Rod to tell her, Rod never did.

Ronnie, on the other hand, had been a girl magnet. He'd dated Rosemary, Linda, and Regina—all at the same time, and not one of them seemed to care. He and Rod alone knew the truth: that he cared for one girl only, the untouchable Darlene Poulardi. Until the night of the junior/senior prom, everyone thought that she'd only dated older boys. The parents of Darlene's date had called two days before the big dance and told her that their son was attacked by four guys while leaving his dorm on the local community college campus. He had been hospitalized with two fractured elbows and would be in the hospital for at least a week. When Ronnie had found out that Darlene no longer had a date to the most important school function of the year, he had called and asked if she would go with him. Ronnie "Don Juan" Parker and Darlene "I know I am fine" Poulardi. With her amazingly tanned complexion and perfect blonde hair, she was a beauty to behold.

The water got cold in the shower, and Rod's mind was brought back to the present. He turned off the shower; it still dripped like it did when he was a kid, and this made him smile. But his mind was still on Darlene. Presumed dead now, for over twenty-three years. Darlene Poulardi went missing on that fateful prom night, Saturday, October 28, 1991.

Right away the suspicion fell on Rod. It seemed the whole town was certain that he had something to do with her disappearance. There was a grand jury hearing and then a preliminary hearing. Rod was given a choice to join the military and leave town, or stand trial. Dobie's father, Donald O'Connor Sr., who was the prosecutor, made it clear to Rod that he should leave town for the sake of his friends, for the sake of the Four.

The Poulardis were outraged after Rod left town, but they were soon pacified once they received the settlement check from the city in the amount of eight hundred thousand dollars. They vowed to use the money to find their daughter, but four months after Rod had joined the military, the Poulardi family also left town. That information was in the last letter he'd received from Mrs. Parker. The last news article he'd received from Rachael's Point eight years into the military, from the *Tribune Pressure Point,* was that Wanda Hall had died of unknown causes on the same date as the night Darlene Poulardi went missing. The story had caught his eye because a note had been found at the crime scene stating, "All will pay."

The local newspaper reported Wanda's death as a cult killing, while observing the death of town beauty Darlene Poulardi. The full-page ad that observed Darlene's death every year was paid for by her parents. The cult killing theory was never proven.

Once again, Rod was jolted from his memories of the past by the telephone ringing. "Ronnie? Ronnie?" Evidently he had not returned. Rod ran downstairs and picked up the phone. "Hello, Parkers residence."

The soft female voice on the other end said, "We need to meet."

"I am sorry, this isn't Ronnie."

"I know. I am talking to Rod Strickland, and we need to meet."

"Who are you?"

"You saw me outside of your window earlier today."

"My God!"

"No, not God, but a messenger," the voice said calmly.

"When? Where do you want to meet?"

"Conley's Restaurant on Main Street, tomorrow at noon."

He said, "I didn't get your name." There was no answer, and the line went dead.

"Rod?" Ronnie had returned and was standing in the doorway. "Who was that?"

"Wrong number."

"Who did they want?"

"I don't know. It was the wrong number."

"Rod?" Ronnie said.

"What?" Now Rod was annoyed.

Backing away from his houseguest, Ronnie feigned embarrassment. "You gonna put some clothes on, man?" Rod had been so startled about the surprise phone call that he had not even noticed that the towel had fallen from his waist. "Oh, shut up!" he said with a laugh. "As soon as I am dressed, I want to go to the cemetery."

"Um," Ronnie began to protest.

"Give me twenty minutes, and I will be ready," Rod said, cutting off Ronnie's protest as soon as it began.

CHAPTER 3

Dusk was upon them as the two men arrived at Benshoff Cemetery, which was outside of Rachael's Point. It sat on a hill above the city and was very well kept by funds from the city and its one groundskeeper. The gravesites were kept clean free of trash and debris. The lawn was immaculate, the headstones were easy to read, and the map at the entrance clearly showed directions to each section of the cemetery. The only problem was there was no lighting in the cemetery; once it got dark, it was almost impossible to find a grave. The only light would be in the groundskeeper's office, which was at the southeast corner of the cemetery.

The cemetery had been started by the Benshoff family, who'd settle there in the 1800s. The first to be buried on the plot of land was David Benshoff in 1834. It was initially a family plot, but as the population grew due to the railroad and steel companies moving to the city, more area was needed for those who were dying. The Benshoff family began selling plots for thirty-four dollars. The selling pitch was, "Keep watch over the city you lived and worked in."

"Let's hurry up so we can get out of here before it gets dark," Ronnie said.

"Afraid?" Rod teased.

"No, but there are no lights here, and I want to make sure that we could find the grave."

When they reached Mrs. Alice Parker's grave, Rod felt overwhelmed. There arose a deep hurt inside of him, and he was not able to hold back his tears. "You should have told me," he said, pulling away from Ronnie.

"I'm sorry."

"Where is Darlene's marker?"

Ronnie pretended to be hard of hearing. "Whose marker?"

"Darlene Poulardi. Remember her?

"Rod, you really want to go to her marker? You just fell apart at Mom's grave."

"I loved your mom. She was like a mother to me. As for Darlene, I did not love or like her. You remember telling the grand jury that?"

"You know that was Dobie's idea!"

"Take me to the grave."

At the marker, Rod read, "Darlene, in hopes of your return." He looked intently at Ronnie. "Whose idea was it to have a grave marker when her body was never found?"

"Mr. O'Connor. He felt that it would bring closure to the matter. He got the city to agree to pay eight hundred thousand to the Poulardis as well, and he convinced the police to stop the investigation. He also talked the Poulardis into the construction of a gravesite. Darlene's family insisted that their daughter's burial place be marked in this way, with words that expressed their hope that she would one day return to them."

As the two men turned to leave, they were startled by a male figure who had come up from behind them. "Whoa!" Ronnie said at the same time Rod was about to land the intruder a lethal blow. He caught himself when he recognized Craig Newman, sole caretaker of Benshoff Cemetery for the last two decades.

Newman was probably in his seventies. While looking at Rod, Newman asked, "Why did you come back? Is it your turn to … is it your turn to appear dead and not die? Your turn to make a pact? It happens every eight years."

Ronnie tugged furiously at Rod's jacket. "Let's go!"

"You know it's true, Ronnie Parker. That Hall girl, Wanda, and even your own mother."

"Shut up, Mr. Newman!" Ronnie said.

The old man grabbed Rod's arm. "Leave town. Don't be here on Saturday night. It is the anniversary every eight years."

"What are you talking about?" Rod was lost.

"Ask your friend Parker. He knows," said Mr. Newman.

Ronnie shook his head. "Rod, I am leaving. Are you coming?"

Rod removed Mr. Newman's hand from his arm and saw there was sorrow in the caretaker's eyes. Again, the old man pleaded, "Leave town! Don't let them get to you!"

In the distance, standing by another grave, a black duster and long blonde hair blew in the wind. As the men drove away, the figure who had watched from afar was now walking toward Mr. Newman, who had gone back to the office and closed up for the night. As the figure neared him, Newman turned his head skyward and whispered into the black starless night, "Lord, I tried."

* * *

The next morning, Rod woke up early, anticipating his meeting with the duster lady at Conley's Restaurant at noon. As he sat in the kitchen that hadn't changed since he was a teenager, he surveyed the white table. It had metal legs and was situated to the left of the gas stove. Then there was the old, white GE refrigerator against the wall that had to be defrosted, that he'd thought was much bigger than it now seemed.

"Ronnie!" he shouted.

"What?"

"I need to use your car."

"For what?" Ronnie asked.

"There are some errands I want to run. I need some items."

"No problem. I can drive you."

"No, thanks. I want to ride around and see who I see, and who sees me."

Forcing a light chuckle at his friend's attempt at being self-absorbed, Ronnie threw the keys at Rod, telling him to remember the reunion meeting of the Four at 8:00 p.m., at Conley's.

Rod left for the restaurant at 11:40 a.m., twenty minutes before he was to meet the angel lady. He had so many questions to ask her, beginning with where she went after stopping the semitrailer truck from killing the school kids.

It was a short drive to Conley's. The temperature was in the high sixties, so Rod put the top down on the 1966 blue GTO. After checking himself in the rearview mirror, Rod decided that he looked okay—not great, but okay.

* * *

As Rod pulled away from the house, Ronnie was inside dialing Dobie's number. "Dobie, we need to talk! Mr. Newman was talking to Rod last night at the cemetery. I don't know whether he believed the old man, but you need to go see him."

Later as he stepped into the shower, Ronnie thought to himself that he would be glad when this was over.

* * *

Conley's was the restaurant where everybody met. For a meeting with a client, Conley's. For a meeting with your wife or lover, also Conley's. And for a meeting with an angel, what better place than Conley's?

Though Rod had no proof, he was sure his mystery lady was an angel. He had spent the last five years on the lecture circuit and on TV, debating with scholars in defense of the existence of angels and their roles as messengers sent to intervene on behalf of mankind, as directed by God. For this reason, many often accused him of being a religious zealot. Rod saw himself as a man who had had a revelation.

On the day of the runaway semi, the divine had come near his soul, and like Nicodemus, who came to Jesus by night, Rod had heard Jesus say, "You must be born again." Well, he'd been born again, and it had happened the night after he saw the angel save the children. When he got home, he had found the Bible that Mrs. Parker had given him. He opened it up to the Book of Revelation and read, "Behold, I stand at the door and knock. If any man hear my voice and open the door, I will come into him and sup with him, and he with me." He then turned to 1 John and read, "If we confess our sins, he is faithful and just to forgive us our sins, and to cleanse us from all unrighteousness." That night, he had fallen on his knees and confessed his sins. He'd asked God for forgiveness and had accepted Jesus as Lord. When he turned in his two-week notice the next day at work, he was still basking in the freedom and liberation that had overcome him the day before. That was when he began his research on angels.

Rod Strickland's radical decision to leave the comfort of secure, full-time employment to embark on a study of angelic beings led him to Dr. John Leventry, the country's leading authority on the subject. Soon thereafter, Dr. Leventry passed on the mantle to his protégé, calling on Rod to conduct all his speaking engagements. Dr. Leventry began to decrease as Rod Strickland began to increase. Rod had never told his mentor about the angel lady he was about to meet.

There was a tap on his shoulder. Rod turned, and there she was. "Hello, my name is Amy." Rod stared at the woman with short brown hair and riveting brown eyes. Her high cheek bones and thin, perky lips, coupled with a long and full neck, gave her the face of an angel. Smiling, she asked him, "Are you all right?"

"Yes, yes, I am fine," Rod said, regaining his composure, "Let's sit."

She looked at him and said, "Would you mind if we didn't eat? I'd like you to take me to Benshoff Cemetery."

Rod was surprised at her request. "Why do you want to go there?"

"You'll see," she said while turning to go.

"Where's your duster?" he asked as he held the door for her.

"In the GTO," she answered with a wink. Far from her signature outfit, Amy wore a long-sleeved, chocolate silk blouse and form-fitting blue jeans with brown hiking boots.

* * *

Amy's brown-on-brown attire did not escape the notice of Don Hart, the city manager, as he watched the couple leave Conley's and get into the convertible.

Losing no time, he dialed Dobie's cell phone. "He's with a woman!" Don blurted out. "I don't know. I never saw her before."

"Okay, I'm on it."

Don's next call was to his office. "Hello, Sara. This is Mr. Hart. I need to know who checked into the Downtown Inn over the last two days. I just need the names of any females. Thank you." He hung up and went to his car. Following Rod and his new friend would not be hard because there was only one way they could have gone without making a U-turn and coming back in his direction.

* * *

While Don started his vehicle and began to follow the route that Rod would be taking, Rod looked over at Amy and asked, "Are you her?"

Her one-word answer was, "Yes."

* * *

After receiving the phone call from Don Hart, Dobie's mind was racing. He got out of his car at Benshoff Cemetery. *What else is going to happen? This was supposed to be easy with no complications. Get Rod into town for a speaking engagement, he dies, and we are good for eight more years. Instead, Strickland gets in town and goes to the cemetery. Crazy Mr. Newman tries to warn him. A strange woman has contacted him, and she could be a danger to the plan. Now Newman is dead. It appears he died less than thirty minutes after Strickland and Ronnie left the cemetery.*

"How am I going to make his death seem like it was from natural causes?" Dobie said out loud to himself.

CSI was already on the scene, and Detective John Smadja was on the case. "Why are you here?" the detective asked Dobie as he was crawling under the police tape.

As usual, Dobie ignored the junior detective. After bending over the deceased, he unzipped the body bag and looked up at the coroner. "Has a cause of death been determined?"

"Not yet. I am going to have to do an autopsy."

Dobie shrugged his shoulders. "Looks like natural causes to me."

From behind him, Dobie heard, "Amazing how you can be so sure, just by looking at his face." When he turned to see the owner of the voice that had spoken from behind him, Dobie stood face-to-face with Rod.

"Rod Strickland, welcome home. But who let you get this close?"

Rod turned and pointed at Detective Smadja.

"He should know better than to let a civilian into a crime scene," Dobie said.

"Oh," Rod replied. "I thought death was by natural causes?"

Dobie gave Rod his famous, intimidating stare that had caused many (including Rod) to back down and change the subject. But Rod was not the least bit threatened, and he stared back at Dobie with a coldness that said, "I will break your back." He had not used that stare since his days in black-ops.

There was total silence until Dr. Maxwell broke it. "Crime scene, natural causes. We won't know anything until I do my thing."

Dobie looked at him. "Let me know as soon as possible."

Detective Smadja interjected, "I will be with him during the autopsy, and I will bring the report to you."

"You do that, Detective," Dobie said.

Rod had not stopped staring at Dobie. "I guess I will see you tonight at eight o'clock," Dobie said in a manufactured pleasant voice.

"I will be there," Rod said.

Dobie's cell phone rang. He turned and answered it as he walked to his car.

Rod turned to Detective Smadja and asked, "Did you find anything in Mr. Newman's office?"

"No ... well, nothing other than a notepad with your name, the name of Angerona, and the date of your lecture, which I must say I am looking forward to hearing. I am a new Christian, and I'm very anxious to know how you can tell for sure if God is intervening in a person's life. It will be interesting to find out if he still uses angels like he did with Daniel, Jacob, and John."

Rod smiled and said, "Oh, you'll know without a shadow of a doubt." He then remembered Amy was still in the car and that Dobie was heading that way. "Excuse me," he said to Detective Smadja as he hurried back to the GTO, wondering what type of conversation Dobie was having with Amy.

"Leaving so soon?" said Dobie. "Don't you want to go through Newman's papers, his desk and drawers?"

Rod relaxed. Evidently, Dobie hadn't seen Amy, or he chose not to speak with her. As a matter of fact, Amy was not in the GTO or anywhere in sight. "Why would I want to do that?" Rod answered.

"Why are you at Benshoff Cemetery?" Dobie shot back. "You were just going to pick up a few things from the store."

Rod realized Ronnie must have revealed his plans to Dobie after he left the house.

"And where is your girlfriend?" Dobie said sarcastically. "I thought you were a Christian. Well, I guess single Christians need companionship on the road."

Rod smiled, refusing to let Dobie rattle him. "First, I have no girlfriend or companion. Second, I came up to see Mr. Newman." As he spoke the words, in his heart he asked for forgiveness for not being totally truthful. "Mr. Newman said that it is my turn to die, but not die—my turn to make the pact. He warned me to leave Rachael's Point. I was coming to ask him about what type of pact I was going to be making, and with whom."

"The old man was delusional!" Dobie said angrily. "I've got to get back to the station. I'll see you tonight."

Rod's eyes followed Dobie to his car. He watched him get in, turn on his siren, and leave in a hurry. That was Dobie's way of showing he was in charge.

Rod was torn between staying at the cemetery to find out more information from Detective Smadja and going back to the house and hopefully seeing Amy before the 8:00 meeting of the Four. After deciding to stay at the cemetery, he asked Detective Smadja to call him if they found anything he could use in his lecture, especially anything on why his name was linked with Angerona, the goddess of death and renewal. The detective, who stood five feet nine inches with sandy blond hair, glasses, and no facial hair, was glad to do whatever he could for the famous Rod Strickland. He also volunteered to call him with the autopsy report.

"Call me before you call Dobie," Rod said. He then paused slightly before continuing. "Also, could you tell me anything about the murder of the former city manager, Carter Michaels? And about twenty-one years ago, there was a murder of a young woman named Wanda Hall."

"That was before I got on the force," Smadja interrupted.

"I know, but see what you can find out from the files," Rod said.

"Do you think we have fallen angels involved in these cases?"

Rod smiled at Detective Smadja and said, "The Bible reminds us that we wrestle not with flesh and blood, but with principalities. So who knows?"

Rod began walking to the GTO, thinking about Amy and where she could have gone. She was standing by the passenger side of the car. "Where did you go?" he gushed.

"That is not important," she said. "We need to get any notes that the groundskeeper had regarding his studies of fallen angels, or any pacts made with supposed deities.

"Why?" he asked.

"Because your life and your future may depend on it."

Frustrated, Rod said, "This is getting a little bit too much for me."

"Why, Rod?" Amy said, staring at him with her soft brown eyes. "You believe in angels. You believe I am an angel. You have studied their appearances. You investigated them, made a determination that they exist, and concluded that they intervene in people's lives as directed by God. You have shared your beliefs, and hundreds of thousands have accepted Christ because of that. So why now are you overwhelmed?"

"Because it seems that for whatever reason I was asked to come home, it is not for good."

Amy touched his arm lightly, looked intently at him, and spoke again in that soft, celestial tone, "They mean it for evil, but God has brought you back home to do good, and to stop evil."

"What evil, Amy?"

"The one that killed Mr. Newman, Carter Michael's, Wanda Hall, and Ronnie's mother."

"How do you know?"

"Trust me on Carter, Mrs. Parker, and Wanda. I have read the death reports as to what occurred."

"What about Mr. Newman?"

Again, those brown eyes bore into his soul and his knees got weak when she said, "I witnessed it."

CHAPTER 4

Ronnie Parker, Don Hart, and Dobie sat in a conference in city hall. This was the meeting before the meeting, and Dobie was in charge. "Shut up!" he told everyone, and then he lowered his voice. "This is not complicated. We meet with Strickland tonight, give him the schedule for the lecture, be sure he is there alone an hour before, and let it happen."

"Rod is different than the others," Ronnie interjected. "He is a Christian."

"So am I!" Don Hart said proudly.

"You are a Christian pimp," Ronnie said sharply.

Don leaned in threateningly. "Who do you think you are, to say that to me?"

"Exactly what I said. You are a Christian pimp. The only time you are a Christian is when there is something in it for you. You pimp the words of the Bible to benefit your goals or schemes. What is your latest slogan? 'Give and it will be given to you'?" People gave, and what did you give back? A new city tax."

Don felt the veins in his neck bulging as he stood up and pushed his chair back, to make room for the beat-down he was about to put on Ronnie. "Who the—"

"Relax, Hart," said Dobie, rising from his chair and looking squarely at Don. "What are you going to do? Besides, Parker is right. You are a pimp. Pimp, politician—they are the same thing." He turned to leave the room but decided he had one more question for Don. "Have you ever considered the similarities between Jesus and Angerona?"

"There aren't any," said Ronnie. "And that's the problem. This is going to be a battle between Rod's Christian beliefs and what we have in store for him."

"Wait," said Don, who had regained his composure. "We have nothing in store for Rod. We agreed to have him here on October 8 for a lecture on angels, a sold-out event. Anything else that happens to him, happens."

"Don, you are not talking to your constituents. We are in a pact with Angerona, the angel of silence," Ronnie said.

Dobie had had enough of their bickering. "Shut up, both of you! Here is the bottom line. This Saturday, October 8, is the twenty-fourth anniversary of what occurred with Darlene Poulardi. Just as she made a pact with Angerona, in order to stay alive, we also made a pact. Every eight years, there has to be a sacrifice. On the twenty-fourth year, it must be one of those who was involved with what was done to Darlene. That means one of us. I am *not* going to be the one. If you or Hart want to volunteer to replace Strickland, speak now."

There was silence; neither Don nor Ronnie spoke.

"I will see you at Conley's at eight o'clock." said Dobie. "The Four reunite again."

As the three walked by one of the manager's office on the way out of the building, an oldies station was playing the old Peaches and Herb song "Reunited." Dobie laughed and whistled the tune, to the displeasure of his friends, who saw no humor in the moment.

CHAPTER 5

Rod and Amy were almost back downtown before he spoke a word. He had driven down Benshoff Hill Road and crossed over the R. P. Memorial Bridge just two miles outside of town, where there were little novelty shops and an ice cream parlor. He finally pulled the GTO over and said, "You witnessed it?"

"Yes."

"Then why didn't you stop it?"

"That is not my assignment. Mr. Newman was destined to die. I was on my way to try to warn him, but ..."

"But what?" Rod asked impatiently.

"He was going to die regardless, Rod. It is appointed to man to die. Please trust me. It was his appointed time. What is more important is what Mr. Newman told you."

Rod started the GTO. "Mr. Newman told me to leave town and not to do the lecture Saturday night. He said that I would be next to die, but not die."

"Good advice," replied Amy. "But you're not leaving, are you?"

"No," Rod said.

"In that case, you need to know who you are going up against."

"Who?"

"Angerona."

"Who is that? That is the second time I have heard that name."

"Mr. Strickland," Amy began to explain. "Angerona is a fallen angel who makes pacts with young, beautiful girls who want to live on and grow in wisdom, but remain young and beautiful."

Rod didn't understand. "What does that have to do with me?"

25

"You need to let me out at the corner," Amy said, as though Rod hadn't asked her a question. "I will be in touch with you, Mr. Strickland." And with that, she got out on the corner of Franklin and Main Street. Rod did not need to look in the rearview mirror because he knew that she would have disappeared. He looked anyway. She was gone.

CHAPTER 6

Rod got back to the Parkers' house and was grateful that Ronnie was not around. He went upstairs and dialed Professor Leventry's cell number. "Professor, I need information on Angerona, a fallen angel. I need to know who she is and whether I should be afraid. Please call me when you get this message."

As he sat in the old folding chair in front of the wooden desk where he used to do his homework, Rod couldn't remember the last time he was afraid. It occurred to him suddenly that he was off schedule since landing at the airport. He had not stopped to give God thanks for a safe trip, and neither had he taken the time to pray and ask for guidance with his lecture. He had not stopped to pray for the people who would be moved by his words, turn to God, ask for forgiveness, and ask Jesus to come into their lives.

Rod had his lecture already prepared, but in five years he had not stuck to his notes. Always he let himself be guided by the Holy Spirit. It also helped him when he had a chance to call and speak with his pastor, Franklin R. Kimble, who always had an insightful and encouraging word for him.

After going into his bedroom now, Rod shut the door behind him. He removed his shoes and outer clothing and prostrated himself before God. For Rod, this was necessary. He believed that it was important to be humble before God, and the shedding of his clothing brought him before God with no pretense. He began in earnest. "Oh, ye who answers prayers."

* * *

Meanwhile, at the Haynes Street Convention Center, a lone figure wearing a duster walked around the center, praying as she went. Amy started, "Lord, you are my strength. No weapon formed against me or the one you have placed in my charge will prosper."

* * *

In Texas, Dr. John Leventry had just finished listening to Rod's message and said to himself, "Yes, Rod, be afraid." He fell on his knees in his office by the oak desk where he and Rod had many discussions, and he prayed. "Oh, ye who answers prayers."

CHAPTER 7

"**D**oc, we need to get this autopsy done now," Detective Smadja said.

Bernie replied, "I am the chief coroner, and I know the importance of the timing of the autopsy, but I also know the importance of my body having food. Please allow me to get a ham and cheese sandwich from the fridge, and we will proceed."

Detective Smadja smiled at the thirty-four-year-old coroner, who stood less than five feet tall but had the smoothest black skin and the biggest ego Smadja had ever seen. Bernie Maxwell was the top graduate in his class, yet instead of going to any one of the national hospitals that were recruiting him, he decided to come to Rachael's Point to be the city's chief corner. He had been in that position now for six years. He was single but was known to have many companions. One never saw him in public without a pretty woman by his side. The joke around city hall was that although Bernie Maxwell was a short man, he was a man's man.

Best of all, he was not intimidated by Chief Detective Donald J O'Connor. In the six years that he had been chief coroner, there had only been one argument with Dobie. No one knew what the argument was about, but it had ended with Dobie going to his father to secure a judge's order to prevent the coroner from doing what he was going to do—and evidently did before the court order was filed. It must have been hard for the district attorney to ask the city's chief coroner to restrain from an action, especially when they were supposed to be on the same side. Dobie tried to get Bernie removed, but his father would not go along with that.

Bernie came back through the doors of the city morgue with sandwich, soda, the body, and the necessary equipment for the autopsy.

He turned to Terri, who had joined him, and Detective Smadja. Still in her early twenties, Terri looked like a Native American but was quick to tell you she was black and proud. "Terri," said Dr. Maxwell, "make sure the body bag is tested for fluid."

"It is being processed, Doctor, and the report will come straight to you," she answered.

The coroner looked at the detective, "Detective Smadja, have you ever witnessed an autopsy?"

"No, sir," was the reply.

"Well, you should leave," Bernie continued. "I don't have time to administer first aid to you when you pass out and hit your head on the floor."

Detective Smadja started to say, "Doc, I think—"

The coroner had climbed onto a special stool, and his eyes were now even with the detective's. "Get out!" he told him. Detective Smadja turned, and as he was leaving, he heard the doctor say, "Come back in two hours. And don't worry—you are the detective on this case and will get the results first." Without turning around, Detective Smadja nodded a thank-you and continued on through the exit door.

CHAPTER 8

Don Hart buzzed his secretary.

"Sir?"

He asked, "Do you have the information on the names of any females who were alone and registered for a room over the last two days?"

"Mr. Hart, there were sixty-three people who checked into the hotel. Twenty were couples, and the other twenty-three were males."

"Thank you, Sandy." He leaned back in his chair, closed his eyes, and tried to pray, but because there was no audience, he could not think of anything to say.

His phone rang. "Yes?"

"Mr. Hart," Sandy said, "there is a problem at the convention center. An intruder was caught as she was stepping off the side of the main building at the convention center."

"Have the police been called?"

"No, sir. Security has her."

"Don't call the police. Let them know that I am on the way." He thought for a second to call Dobie and Parker, but he changed his mind. *I can handle this. I am the city manager.*

CHAPTER 9

Rod stepped out of the shower. His time in worship refreshed and filled his soul and spirit, and it also gave him strength. He agreed with the psalmist that said, "God is my exceeding joy." He got dressed: blue oxford shirt, brown khaki pants, brown socks, and brown loafers. He loved the classic look.

He looked at his cell phone, and there were two messages from Pastor Kimble and Dr. Leventry. He called the pastor first. The conversation was brief but powerful, as usual. Pastor Kimble told Ronnie the importance of staying in the boat, reminding him of the story in Matthew when Jesus told the disciples, "Let's get into the boat and go to the other side." The key of course was the fact that Jesus said *they* were going to the other side. In the middle of the trip, a violent storm arose while Jesus was asleep in the back of the boat. The frightened disciples, unable to bail the water out of the sinking vessel fast enough, woke up Jesus. He rebuked the wind, instantly bringing peace and calm back to the sea. According to Pastor Kimble, these friends of Jesus had it all wrong. The wind, and not the waves, was the real problem.

Pastor Kimble said, "Rod, be sure to focus on the actual problem, not on the peripheral occurrences. Stay in the boat." He then prayed for Rod and told him he would see him on his return to Dallas.

Rod called Dr. Leventry next. The doctor said, "Rod, I have been waiting for your call. Son, how are you involved with Angerona?"

"I am not," Rod said, "but my name has been linked to hers. What can you tell me about her?"

"Do you want the full story, or the *Reader's Digest* version?" Doctor Leventry asked.

"I have a dinner engagement in a few hours, so the *Reader's Digest* version."

Dr. Leventry was brilliant but could turn a two-sentence answer into a forty-five-minute lecture. Rod could not have been as successful as he was today without God placing the professor in his life. Dr. Leventry's partially bald head reminded Rod of Mel Cooley, the producer of the old *Dick Van Dyke Show*. The doctor wore glasses like the character and even had the same serious look. It was clear to everyone, though, that Dr. Leventry loved the Lord— all six feet, two inches of him. When he spoke about God's mercy, grace, and goodness, he did so passionately and with the spirit of a humble servant. He always used his favorite scripture when he felt himself getting upset, or if Rod got upset. "Remember," Dr. Leventry would say, "while we were yet in sin, Jesus died for the ungodly." Then he would tell his protégé, "Relax. We've got this, with the help of the Master."

On the phone, Doctor Leventry told Rod, "Angerona is a fallen angel, one who fell with Satan from heaven. This angel took the form or character of a goddess during the time of the Roman Empire. They named her the goddess of the winter solstice. She has power over young females, who revere and appease her in all sorts of ways because they're convinced Angerona can keep them looking youthful well past their deaths."

"Are they vampires?" Rod asked.

"No, they are vain, young girls who want to look seventeen or eighteen all of their lives. These worshippers of Angerona will normally move from city to city, not staying too long in any one place because they must return every eight years to the city where the pact was made, to take the life of the one who tried to kill her, or that of a substitute. However, on the third cycle, the twenty-fourth year, the person or persons involved in the murder of the young girl must die."

Rod wanted to say, *This is ridiculous*. But he knew if Dr. Leventry was telling him this, it was based upon fact. Instead, he asked, "How are the victims killed?"

"By a word whispered in the ear of the victim that causes such great anger or fear he has a massive stroke and die. The death appears to be of natural causes, but a close examination will show that there is no cadaver fluid." Rod didn't know what that meant, and he didn't ask.

"So, Rod," Dr. Leventry asked again, "how are you connected with Angerona?"

CHAPTER 10

The chief coroner came out of the morgue with a concerned look on his face. "What's the problem, Doc? What's the cause of death?" Detective Smadja asked as he followed Bernie into his office.

The older man climbed upon a stool and pulled a mythology book off the crowded cherry oak shelf. He went to his desk, placed the book down, went to the table of contents, and there it was. The name *Angerona* was number eighteen on the list of Roman gods and goddesses; they were listed in alphabetical order.

"Doc, cause of death?" Detective Smadja repeated.

"Natural cause, with help," came the pensive reply.

"What?" the detective asked.

"Detective Smadja, have a seat. Mr. Craig Newman had a massive stroke."

"Okay," Smadja said while sitting down.

"Detective, what do you know about the brain and strokes?"

"Very little" was the reply.

"Well, the brain has three primary components," Bernie continued. "There is the cerebrum, the largest portion, which controls a number of higher functions such as speech, emotions, and the fine control of movement. Second, there is the cerebellum, which is the second largest area; it controls reflexes, balance, and certain aspects of movement and coordination. Then there's the brain stem, which is responsible for a variety of automatic functions; it is critical to life such as breathing, digestion, heartbeat, and the state of being awake."

Bored, Detective Smadja interrupted, "What does this have to do with—"

"Let me finish, Detective," the chief coroner said. "A stroke can and does occur in any of these areas, but it is rare for a stroke to occur in all areas at the same time." Bernie sat back, took a breath, and said, "I have seen this twice since I have been here in Rachael's Point, and my predecessor's reports show that it has happened two other times in the last sixteen years."

"Okay," Detective Smadja said, showing that he understood the anomaly, "but what did you mean by death by natural causes, with help?"

Leaning forward with his elbows on the desk, his short, index fingers resting on both temples, Bernie began. "There are studies that report the only way for this to happen is for a person to have the emotion of anger or fear, or a type of mental stress that triggers such an effect on the circulation of the blood in a body or the nervous system so that the brain is overloaded. Blood clotting occurs, and all systems shut down. The brain, in layman's terms, shuts down completely."

"I have two questions," Detective Smadja said. He took out his pen and notebook. "Who caused this to happen to Mr. Newman, and who were the other three people who died in the same manner?"

"Before I answer," Bernie said, "I need a drink."

"Doc, I need you sober."

"Relax, Detective." Bernie got out of the chair, walked over to the small refrigerator, and got an orange soda. "Would you like one?"

"No, thank you."

Bernie went back to his desk, settled in the chair, grabbed the book, and turned it around so that the detective could read it. He pointed to the eighteenth chapter: Angerona.

"Doc?"

"Angerona is the answer to the first question you asked. The answer to question number two is City Manager Carter Michaels, Mrs. Gloria Parker, and Wanda Hall."

"Why wasn't any of this reported?" Smadja asked.

"I was ordered by the court not to release my findings on Carter Michaels."

"That was the big argument you had years ago with Dobie."

"Partly," Bernie said. "He didn't even want an autopsy, but I'd already done it before the court order was issued. Detective Smadja, something ungodly has been going on—and still is—in Rachael's Point."

The detective looked down again at the name Angerona and asked, "Who is Angerona, and why do you think this person has anything to do with any of the deaths?"

CHAPTER 11

As the coroner was explaining his Angeronian theory to Detective Smadja, City Manager Don Hart arrived at the Hayne's Street Convention Center. The five-thousand-seat center was sold out for the celebrated lecturer, hometown boy Rod Strickland. Twenty-four years ago, many of the residents in Rachael's Point believed Rod had got away with the murder of Darlene Poulardi, who was Ronnie's prom date. However, Don knew he did not get away with murder because there never was a murder. Well, there was a murder, but no death.

Don Hart walked into the security wing of the convention center, where they were holding the intruder. He opened the door and was surprised. Sitting in a cloth-covered folding chair between two security guards was the woman he had seen leaving Conley's with Rod Strickland. "Hello," Don said in his *I am Don Hart, city manager* voice.

"Hello," Amy said.

"What's your name?"

"Amy."

"Amy what?"

"Just Amy."

"Well, Just Amy, why were you marking off the parameter of the center? Is this a prelude or surveillance for your friends who will be coming to demonstrate against Strickland?"

"No. I was walking around the building and praying for Mr. Strickland."

"Praying for what?" Don smirked.

Amy looked Don Hart straight in the eye. "I was praying for his strength and safety, and my strength to stand up against Angerona."

Don Hart looked as if he had been kicked in the solar plexus; all the color drained out of his face. Amy, who was sitting in the chair beside the metal desk in the security room, said, "Mr. Hart, you need to release me so this does not get too far out of hand."

Don looked up at the security guards who were in the room with him. They looked back at him, shrugging their shoulders.

"Mr. Hart, release me," Amy said again. "You do not have to be part of this."

"Part of what?" The voice belonged to Dobie O'Connor, who had just entered the room.

A visibly shaken Don Hart was at a loss for words as Dobie announced that Amy was under arrest, and he ordered the security guards to take her to the holding office downstairs.

"On what charge, sir?" the shorter of the two guards asked.

"Trespassing, you idiot!" barked Dobie, glaring at the man.

Without any further questions or comments, the guards took hold of Amy and began leading her away. As she passed by Dobie, she said to him quietly, "I will see you Saturday night."

Then as soon as she was out of earshot, Dobie turned to Hart and asked, "Why didn't you call me? Who is this woman?"

Don, seated in the chair behind the desk, said, "Dobie, this was the woman I saw with Strickland—and she knows." Looking up from the desk, with his voice trembling, he asked, "Are we going to get through this?"

Dobie gave a one-word answer: "Yes." As he walked out, he added under his breath, "At least, I will."

CHAPTER 12

Rod and Ronnie were sitting in the living room and looking at old pictures of themselves and of Ronnie's mother when his cell phone rang. It was Detective Smadja.

Rod said, "Ronnie, I need to take this call."

"No problem," Ronnie replied. "I am going to get ready for the meeting of the Four."

"What do you have for me, Detective?" Rod asked, after making sure Ronnie had gotten far enough down the hall.

After listening to all that Detective Smadja said, Rod agreed to meet him and the chief coroner at the morgue. He started to go upstairs to tell Ronnie he has to go out for a while, but Ronnie's cell phone rang, and Ronnie had left on the end of the table. Rod was going to answer it but saw in the caller ID that it was Dobie. He put the cell phone back on the end table and wrote a quick note. "See you at Conley's." He put the note on top of the phone. Ronnie was singing in the shower. Rod smiled at his tone-deaf friend's attempt to sing. He walked out of the house and left in the GTO.

CHAPTER 13

It took Rod ten minutes to get from Ronnie's house to the morgue. He parked the GTO in the parking lot designated for staff and went through the double doors to the elevator that would take him down to the coroner's office. There was a security officer on duty. "May I help you, sir?"

Before Rod could answer, the elevator door opened, and Detective Smadja appeared. "He's with me, Bill."

Rod stepped into the elevator and said nothing. He understood that the coroner would be the one to explain the cause of death. The elevator stopped, and when the doors opened, Rod felt a wisp of cold air. The temperature in the basement where the morgue was located felt like it was twenty degrees lower than in the lobby. The coroner's office was down a long hall and was the last door on the left. As he and Detective Smadja walked, all that could be heard were their footsteps on the tile floor.

Rod thought that there would be a lot of activity going on: moving of corpses, family identifying bodies, and even the sound of equipment being used during an autopsy. He then reminded himself this was Rachael's Point not the city morgue in Dallas, Texas.

They found Bernie Maxwell in his office, stepping off a stool with a book under his arm. "Mr. Strickland, good to see you again," he said.

"Doctor, can you please explain to me the cause of death?" Rod asked.

After settling into his chair, the coroner replied, "Mr. Newman had a stroke that affected every component of his brain. Something scared him to death."

"Something?" Rod asked.

"Mr. Strickland, you lecture about angels, right?"

"Right," Rod replied cautiously, not knowing where this was going.

"Do you believe what you say in your lecture?"

"Of course."

The chief coroner folded his small hands over the open book of mythology and asked, "Are there fallen angels that have the ability to make agreements with humans and grant them extended life?"

"Wait a minute," Detective Smadja interrupted, "this is not sci-fi time."

"No, it's not!" the coroner shot back. "It's reality time."

"Why are you asking these questions?" Rod asked. "What does Mr. Newman's death have to do with fallen angels?"

"A fallen angel was the cause of death for Mr. Newman. The angel who has the ability to whisper in his ear, and the stress of that whisper caused the unprecedented stroke. The cause of death, Mr. Strickland, is natural causes with the help of Angerona." Still staring at Rod, the coroner continued, "Now, what is *your* connection to Angerona?"

Detective Smadja once again interrupted. "Dr. Maxwell, this is out of line. This is not the time or—"

Rod placed his hands on the detective's shoulders and said, "Relax, Detective." He turned to the coroner and said calmly, "There are fallen angels. The Bible verifies that. It appears that Angerona is that fallen angel with whom some others and I made a deal some twenty-four years ago. It appears that she actually has a covenant with a young girl and possibly three young men. Were there any body fluids found in Mr. Newman?"

"I don't have the report yet," the doctor said and reached for his phone. "Terri?" he said, when his secretary answered. "What are the test results of the fluids on the body bag?" After hanging up with Terri, Dr. Maxwell turned his attention back to the two men in his office. "There is no sign of body fluid."

"I have to go," Rod said. "Does Dobie know the results?"

"No. Detective Smadja insisted on telling you first."

"Good. I am going to be meeting with him shortly."

"I need to complete my report," the coroner said. "What should I put as the cause of death?"

"Death by Angerona," was Rod's confident reply.

Detective Smadja said almost to himself, "You should probably change the cause of death on the city manager's death certificate, as well as Gloria Parker's and Wanda Hall's."

Rod stopped suddenly. "All four died with the same symptoms?" Detective Smadja and Bernie Maxwell nodded their heads.

Minutes later, when Rod got off of the elevator in the lobby, he did not hear the security guard say, "Good night." He got to the GTO, opened the door, and put the key in the ignition, but he didn't turn the key for a while. Overcome by emotion, he put his head on the steering wheel. "Oh, God, I know you answer prayers. I know you are a merciful and forgiving God. Please have mercy on me, and forgive me of my sins, especially the one I committed twenty-four years ago that took the lives of four people. Please forgive me. Please, in Jesus's name." He lifted his head from the steering wheel, and his hand shook as he turned the key. He noticed the time on the clock. It was 7:59 p.m.—time for the meeting of the Four.

CHAPTER 14

Rod pulled into the parking lot of Conley's Restaurant after a five-minute drive from the city morgue. When he thought about it there were no two destinations in Rachael's Point that were more than ten minutes apart, except the cemetery on Benshoff Hill, which was twenty minutes from downtown.

Rachael's Point was the home of the Rachael's Point Pirates. The football team was in the past a powerhouse of Western Pennsylvania football. It was a booming steel town like any other in Western Pennsylvania. After the steel mills closed and the jobs moved overseas, the hospital became the largest employer in Rachael's Point. The high school was still there, but the football team was no longer a powerhouse.

The county courthouse was there, which provided training ground for attorneys. Once the attorneys gained experience in the DA's office or in the office of a civil attorney who was trying to find that one big case, they would move on to a big city, either Philadelphia or Pittsburgh.

As he sat in the GTO in Conley's parking lot, parked beside Dobie's police car, Rod thought, *Rachel's Point has the honor of welcoming home Rod Strickland, gifted lecturer and noted authority on the subject of angels— and the one who got off when everyone knew he murdered that girl and hid the body.*

"Yeah, don't forget that part of his biography," Rod said out loud.

He looked at his watch: 8:04 p.m. Time for the showdown. While talking to the coroner, Rod had decided that he would tell Don Hart, Dobie O'Connor, and Ronnie Parker about the night Darlene Poulardi disappeared. He knew what he had done, but he only could guess what had happened after he left her in the cemetery. One of the three had killed

Darlene and hid the body, or maybe all three did. He would make them explain the deaths of Mrs. Parker, Wanda Hall, and Mr. Newman, as well as Carter Michaels. He would tell them that he knew about Angerona, and that he was not going to enter into a pact with a fallen angel. He would let them know the results of the autopsy, adding that he would be going to the federal authorities. There will be a lecture on angels, but all three men would be in jail during the lecture. Rod got out of the GTO, locked the door, and headed for the door of Conley's Restaurant.

CHAPTER 15

As Amy was sitting in the jail cell at the police station, she thought it was interesting that no arrest photos were taken of her, and neither was she fingerprinted. This meant one thing: she was not meant to be part of the general prison population. She heard the guard coming as he was making his rounds. He asked when he came to her cell, "Can I get you anything?"

She smiled and looked at him. "No, Officer Taylor, but thank you."

The officer was taken aback. "How did you know my name?"

"Your name is on the Bible you are carrying." Officer Taylor quickly placed the Bible under the newspaper he was carrying. "Don't be ashamed."

"I'm not," he said. "It is against the rules to have a Bible or any book with you while making cell checks."

"Do you believe what the Bible says, Officer Taylor? Do you believe if you surrender your heart to Jesus and ask him for forgiveness, you will have eternal life with him in heaven?"

He looked at her to determine if she was going to make fun of him. "I want to, but no. I don't have the faith," he said quietly.

"Would you like to have that security?" continued Amy. "You and your whole family."

"I have to go."

As he was walking away, Amy told the guard, "Read John 3:16 and Romans 10:9–10, and then come back and see me." She paused for a second. "Officer Taylor?"

"Yes," he said.

"I will only be here for two more hours. Please come back, and let's pray together before I leave."

Officer Taylor thought to himself, *How did she know we were moving her to county tonight?* He turned and moved on to the next cell.

Amy went back and sat on the bed and prayed. "Oh, Father, bless him. Let him receive you before he dies tonight."

CHAPTER 16

Officer Kerry Taylor, the twin brother of chief coroner's assistant Terri Taylor, had been on the police force for four years. As a good cop who follows the rules, Kerry Taylor was proud of never having accepted anything for free, not even a donut. He considered himself a good person. That was why it is difficult for him to see why he would not go to heaven. He knew many of his Christian colleagues on the force could not say the same, because they were in the habit of taking favors for a favor. Not writing a parking ticket in exchange for tickets to a Penn State football game, for example.

Kerry would never do that. If one deserved a ticket, then one got a ticket, regardless of who one was—even if one was the district attorney's driver. How could he, someone who had better morals and was more honest than many Christians, miss heaven? It did not make sense. His wife and twin sister tried to explain that all of his honesty and righteousness was like filthy rags before God. They challenged him to study the Bible and compare himself with Jesus. At first he thought they were crazy, but every day when he came home from work, his wife would ask him, "How did you measure up today?"

Finally, Kerry started reading the Bible, concentrating on Jesus's deeds as portrayed in the Gospels. He called it the red word study. He thought it was great that all of Jesus's words were in red. This made it easy for him to follow Jesus's life.

Six weeks into his study, Officer Taylor admitted to his wife and sister that he could never measure up to the Lord Jesus. "That's why you need a savior," his sister had told him. But Officer Taylor was not totally convinced, and he did not accept Jesus as his Lord and Savior. He told himself that even though he could not measure up to Jesus, he was still better than the self-proclaimed Christians with whom he worked. He concluded that if they were to go to heaven, he would be there also. He did not need a savior, but a guide to teach him more of the principles and lifestyle of Jesus. That way, the more he imitated Jesus, the better chances he had of going to heaven.

Officer Taylor finished checking all of the jail cells. He went back to the office and found his buddy, Officer Calvin Lee, still sitting at the table, drinking what was probably his eighth cup of coffee in four hours. "I'm going to take fifteen," Taylor announced.

"Take your time. Nothing is happening here," Lee replied.

Kerry Taylor liked to take his evening breaks on the roof of the police department building, under the stars. Tonight as he stood there enjoying the crisp October night air, he felt at peace as he beheld the wonder of God. He could concentrate on God's Word.

That peace was broken by a voice from behind him. "Hello, Officer Taylor. My name is Darlene Poulardi."

"How? And what are you doing up here?" the officer asked, struggling to find his voice. Darlene moved closer, and though he did not know why, he placed his hand on his weapon and stepped back.

Darlene did not take another step but said in a knowing voice, "Tonight is your night. Tonight I will tell you the secret of Angerona, the goddess of beginnings." Officer Taylor said nothing, and so Darlene continued, "You have been seeking someone to guide you through the Bible. I will guide you, and Angerona will sustain you. Let me whisper the secret in your ear." Officer Taylor removed his hand from his weapon and walked toward Darlene. She beckoned him to come near. "Come near, Kerry Taylor. Let me whisper in your ear. Let me be your guide to Angerona."

Kerry Taylor was one step away from Darlene when he heard his name. "Kerry? Kerry, are you up there?" Officer Taylor looked to the woman in front of him, whose face had gone from soft and inviting to angry and cold.

Upon recognizing his twin sister's voice, the officer called back, "Yes, I'm up here." He turned his head as Terri Taylor came out of the door and onto the roof. "It's getting crowded up here," he said nervously, prompting a quizzical look from his sister. He hadn't seen Darlene Poulardi leave. No wonder Terri was looking at him as if he had lost his mind.

"Everything all right, Kerry?" she asked.

"I don't know, Terri. What do you want?"

"Nothing," she said. "It has been an interesting night at the morgue."

"How so?" he asked.

"Well, you know Mr. Newman, the caretaker at the cemetery? They did an autopsy, and Dr. Maxwell asked me to check for body fluids on the bag that he was in. There were no body fluids."

"That's unusual, sis."

"Unusual? It's impossible!" she shouted, remembering how her boss had made a joke about the whole thing. "Dr. Maxwell said it was the curse of someone named Angerona."

Officer Taylor looked at the spot where Darlene had stood, "Terri, remember the stories about Darlene Poulardi?"

"Yes, why?"

"No reason," he said. "No reason. Let's get off this roof."

CHAPTER 17

Rod arrived at Conley's Restaurant and was welcomed with cheers and thunderous applause. Rod was deeply moved and surprised at the reception. There was a huge banner that said, "Welcome home, Rod!" Standing in the middle of the crowd and leading the cheers were Don, Dobie, and Ronnie. Rod was overwhelmed. In the five years that he had been on the lecture circuit, he had never experienced such a reception. He had received standing ovations after a speech, but nothing like this. He was overcome with emotions. He had thought this was just going to be a meeting of the Four.

Rod heard his favorite song, "I'm So Proud" by Curtis Mayfield and the Impressions. He recalled that as a teenager, he'd listened to this song on Mrs. Parker's eight track. Tears filled his eyes. Suddenly, Angerona, fallen angels, unexplained deaths, and autopsy reports did not seem that important. He was home, he was welcomed, and he was loved.

The Four hugged. "We love you, Rod," Ron said.

"Glad you're here," said Don. "Your lecture is a sellout and has been for weeks."

Dobie placed Rod's hand in both of his, gave a look of gratitude, and said sincerely, "I am so happy you came back home. You are a lifesaver."

No sooner had they sat down at their table that a stream of well-wishers came by. Some wanted Rod's autograph, and others wanted their pictures taken with him. "Well, my friend," Ronnie said, "how does it feel to be a celebrity?" Rod did not answer and just smiled. However, inside he felt great.

The last person to come to the table was District Attorney Donald J.

O'Connor Sr. Smiling, the older man shook Rod's hand and said, "I guess time heals all wounds. Welcome home, Rod."

Rod did not reply. In his heart, he had forgiven the man who had made him a scapegoat for a crime he'd not committed. There was nothing more to be said now.

Rod looked over at Dobie and noticed that the younger O'Connor appeared uncomfortable, if not guilty. Don and Ronnie, on the other hand, had their heads down, and neither one looked at him or at Mr. O'Connor.

"Okay, Dad, let us eat," said Dobie, breaking the silence around them.

"Son," Mr. O'Connor said still holding Rod's hand, "I am still the father; you are the son. Keep that in mind. I am still the DA, and you are the policeman."

"Dad," Dobie tried to interrupt.

"I am still holding the cards," continued Mr. O'Connor. There "is no statute of limitations on—"

"Dad!" Dobie shouted, drawing attention from nearby patrons.

"Welcome home, Rod," said the district attorney, ignoring his son and making those his last words before walking out of the restaurant.

"I am sorry, Rod," Dobie said, and he looked sincere.

"That's okay, Dobie. It had to come up eventually. If not now, probably by one of the demonstrators who will be at the seminar."

Just then a hush came over the restaurant. It grew so quiet you could hear the silence.

"Oh, no!" said Ronnie, who was sitting next to Rod.

"Oh, no, what?" Dobie asked.

Dobie turned and repeated what Ronnie said. "Oh, no!" Walking toward their table was Mr. and Mrs. Darryl and Antoinette Poulardi. Dobie looked at the owner of Conley's. Rod stood as Mr. and Mrs. Poulardi reached the table. Mrs. Poulardi spoke first. "So this is how they treat a murderer," she said bitterly. "They give him a welcome-home celebration. I have one question for you, Mr. Strickland. Have you repented for killing our daughter? I read that you are a Christian. Have you repented for killing my daughter? Have any of the angels you lecture about told you where the body of my daughter is? Have you told the angels? If you can't admit to killing my daughter, just tell us what you did with her body!"

Dobie took Mrs. Poulardi's arm to escort her out of the restaurant, but Rod held up his hand, signaling for Dobie to leave her alone. "Mr. and Mrs. Poulardi, I have asked for forgiveness for my part in your daughter's disappearance. But I did not kill your daughter, and I did not do anything to cause her death. I don't know what happened to her body."

Mr. Poulardi put his arm around his wife, looked at the Four, and said words that made Rod feel worse than anything Mrs. Poulardi had said. "Shame on you. Shame on you for what all of you did to my daughter." With that, he escorted his wife out of the restaurant.

The loud chatter in the restaurant had now turned to private conversations and whisperings. People were no longer as welcoming as they had been when Rod first arrived; now they looked at him with condemnation. Except for the customers who were either not alive twenty-four years ago or who were too young to understand what had occurred back then, the patrons felt embarrassed that they had forgotten about Darlene Poulardi's murder, embarrassed that they had been celebrating the man who was implicated in her death.

Rod looked at Dobie, Don, and Ronnie. "Guys, I need to know what happened to Darlene after I left her in the cemetery."

CHAPTER 18

Mr. Poulardi had just opened the passenger door of the car for his wife when they heard a voice that caused them to freeze. "Mother, Dad." They turned and saw their daughter stepping out of the shadows. Mrs. Poulardi found it hard to catch her breath. Her husband's knees became weak, and he had to hold on to the door of their car.

As Darlene walked toward her parents, they saw she wore a long black duster coat, jeans, and black boots, and her long blonde hair flowed over her shoulders. What was more, she still looked seventeen years old.

Mrs. Poulardi went to her daughter and put her arms around her to make sure she was real and not an illusion. Darlene did not return the hug; instead, she whispered into her mother's ear. Mrs. Poulardi's face became a mixture of fear and pain. She turned to her husband and tried to speak, but she fell face first onto the paved parking lot.

Mr. Poulardi heard the bones in his wife's face shatter as it hit the pavement. He looked at Darlene, who was smiling. "Who are you?" he shouted with a mixture of anger and fear.

"I'm your daughter, Dad."

"How have you stayed so young? You should be forty-one, not seventeen!"

"Dad!" Darlene exclaimed. "I've found something so wonderful. I will stay seventeen forever, but I have the wisdom and knowledge of a forty-one-year-old. I am forty-one, but I will always look seventeen."

Darryl Poulardi looked at his wife and then back at his daughter. "Darlene, help me with your mother. I need to go back inside the restaurant and get help."

"Dad, she's dead," Darlene said with no emotion in her voice or on her face.

Mr. Poulardi ignored his daughter. "We need to get help!" he said while choking back tears.

"Dad, she's dead!" the girl repeated.

Her father looked up at her and asked again, "Who are you? You are not my daughter! Who are you?" Mr. Poulardi's voice, which sounded like that of a wounded animal, had drawn the attention of onlookers. Recognizing this, Darlene crouched down by her father, who was holding the head of her dead mother in his arms. "I am your daughter, Dad," she said with urgency. "Come with me, meet my new mother, and live forever." Darlene was smiling now. "Mother had to die. She would have never accepted Angerona's demands. Dad, you are the one with the open mind. You will embrace Angerona once you meet her."

Mr. Poulardi gently laid his wife's bloody head on the pavement and stood up to face his estranged daughter. Darlene stood with him with an expectancy that he understood what she had said, "Dad?"

At six foot three, Darryl Poulardi had white hair that was always neatly combed straight back. He was sixty-three years old but looked forty-three. Yes, he was open-minded, and he embraced all religions though he practiced none. However, the tragedy that was unfolding around him was more than he could stand. His daughter, whom he'd believed for many years to be dead, had come back from the grave and somehow murdered her mother, his wife, right in front of him. Now she was trying to convince him to meet some entity named Angerona, the person she said had given her immortal life.

"Dad, come on," said Darlene, reaching for her father's hand.

Her touch enraged him, and he began yelling at the top of his lungs. "Help! Help! My wife has been murdered!"

"Oh, Dad," Darlene said with genuine sorrow, and she turned to whisper in his ear. Mr. Poulardi died just as suddenly as his wife. When the parking lot attendant got to the scene, all he saw were two dead bodies lying on the pavement, Mrs. Poulardi on her back and Mr. Poulardi facedown.

CHAPTER 19

Inside Conley's, Rod was waiting for answers.

"Ronnie, the plan was for me and Wanda to meet you and Darlene at the cemetery. Once we got there, you were going to pretend that you had gotten very sick. You would see Wanda and me in the car and ask if I could take Darlene home, and Wanda would drive you home. That went off without any problems. Once we switched cars, you and Wanda drove off, leaving me and Darlene with the GTO. When Darlene and I walked back to the GTO, Don, you, and Dobie were there.

"We agreed that the two of you would pretend to knock me out and take Darlene. You were going to tie her to a head stone. You said you would take off her dress and then call the newspaper. You said that you both would be wearing hoods so she could not identify you. I left the cemetery after you took her away and drove home. The next thing I knew, the police were at my door, arresting me for the disappearance of Darlene Poulardi. What happened when I left the cemetery?"

Don started to speak, but Dobie interrupted him. "Strickland, that's what *we* want to know. We went to where you said you left her, and she was not there. We saw you leave the cemetery, and it looked like you had her in the GTO with you. Rod, what did you do with her? Strickland, we are the Four. Tell us where you hid the body. I promise I won't arrest you."

Rod looked at Don and asked, "What were you going to say?"

"Nothing. She was gone."

"Tell me about Angerona!" demanded Rod.

They all froze. "How do you know about her?" asked Don with a tremor in his voice.

"I know she had something to do with the deaths of Wanda Hall, Ronnie's mother, Carter Michaels, and Mr. Newman."

"Don't be ridiculous!" Dobie said.

Rod held his ground. "Dr. Maxwell doesn't think it's ridiculous, and I think he has enough evidence to call in the FBI."

"The FBI!" Ronnie shouted.

"We need to get an autopsy," Dobie and Rod said at the same time.

There was a disturbance at the front of the restaurant. Mr. Conley was speaking to the parking lot attendant. He came over to Dobie and whispered something in his ear. Dobie then shared the news of the deaths of Darryl and Antoinette Poulardi, saying it appeared they'd died of natural causes.

As the Four left the restaurant, Dobie said to Rod, "There have been three deaths since you and your friend arrived in Rachael's Point."

"What friend?" Rod asked.

"The one I have in jail for trespassing at the convention center. The one Don saw you with earlier today. She says her name is Amy."

Rod was honestly confused when he asked, "Dobie, why was she at the convention center?"

"I don't know. She said she was praying," Dobie answered, clearly not believing the story.

Once they reached the parking lot, Dobie knelt by the bodies of Mr. and Mrs. Poulardi, and he noted the look of fear on their faces. He pulled out his cell phone and called Officer Lee, telling him about the Poulardis and instructing him to contact the coroner's office. "I need an officer down here now to handle onlookers," he added. Dobie then turned to his friends. "You guys can leave. I have to wait for an officer and the coroner to arrive."

Don and Ronnie turned to leave.

"I'm staying," said Rod, sensing that something wasn't right. "Dobie, you are right. Three deaths since I have been here, and all three people had some connection to Darlene Poulardi."

"Let it go, Rod," said Ronnie.

"No, I will not let it go! Dobie, you may want these deaths to be ruled as natural causes, but we all know there is more to what is going on."

Dobie was not about to entertain Rod's thoughts. "If you don't leave right now, I will have to arrest you."

"Then how would you explain the death of three citizens caused by Angerona?" asked Rod, unmoved by Dobie's threats.

"Dobie!" Ronnie jumped in. "We need to tell him."

Dobie glared at Ronnie.

"Let me handle it," Ronnie pleaded.

"Okay. Just handle it away from here."

"Come on, Rod, Don. Let's go back to the restaurant."

"By the way," Dobie said to Rod, "what is Amy's last name?"

Rod smiled, "I don't think she has one. She is an angel that has been assigned to protect me."

CHAPTER 20

Officer Calvin Lee was on his way to the roof when the two men met in the hall. He told him about the deaths and that Detective O'Connor wanted him at the restaurant for crowd control.

"Calvin, what do you know about Darlene Poulardi?" Officer Taylor asked.

"Gee," Calvin replied. "She was the daughter of the Poulardis."

Officer Taylor asked if anyone had contacted her.

"Can't," said Officer Lee. "She has been dead for over twenty years."

"Are you sure?"

"Yes, I'm sure."

Terri had come around the corner and joined them as he said, "That's strange." He paused, looked at his twin sister, and then looked at Officer Lee. "That's strange," he said again. "I just met Darlene Poulardi on the roof."

* * *

Detective Smadja was in the chief coroner's office when the coroner received the call on his cell phone. "I will be right there," the doctor said into the cell phone. He then called Terri and told her to meet him in the parking lot at Conley's. Apparently, she already knew about the two bodies that were found there.

"What's going on, Doctor?" Detective Smadja asked.

"Two dead bodies in Conley's parking lot," the chief coroner said as he grabbed his kit.

"What happened?"

"I don't know," said Dr. Maxwell as they got on the elevator, "but I would place money on death by natural causes with help. There is something not of God in this town, and it came with Rod Strickland!"

"I think you're wrong," said Detective Smadja.

The chief coroner looked up at him with a quizzical expression.

"I believe something evil has come to Rachael's Point," continued the detective, "but I believe it came *for* Strickland, not with him."

The two men stepped out of the elevator and went out the lobby door in silence. They both felt uneasy and unsure of what they would find in the parking lot at Conley's.

"Let's take my car," Detective Smadja said.

Terri told her brother that she wanted to ride over to Conley's with him; and she would get her vehicle later. He told her it was against regulations for her to be in the squad car, especially while he was on official business. Besides, Detective O'Connor would be at the scene, and he did not want to have to explain why his sister was riding with him.

Terri protested, "I'm on official business! The chief coroner has asked me to meet him at the scene."

"Okay, let's go," Kerry said, changing his mind. "Officer Lee, we will move the prisoner to county when I return."

"I will be here when you get back," Officer Lee said with a smile in his voice.

As they left, Terri said "Kerry"

"Yeah, sis?"

"You need to accept Jesus now."

"We are on our way to a scene with two dead bodies, and you want to talk about Jesus?"

"Yes," Terri said softly as her brother started the car. "There have been three deaths today. Mr. Newman's was not of natural causes. Something is not right. We need the blood of Jesus to protect us."

"You already have it." Kerry said to his sister. "I don't need it. I am an honest and good man. God will not send anyone good to hell."

He pulled the squad car to the side of Conley's building. A small crowd of about thirteen people were gathered in the parking lot. On the other side of the crowd was Detective O'Connor with the city's only television station, WCNE 5, making a statement. Kerry wondered how the media got there so fast. "Thank you. Thank you, no more questions," said Detective O'Connor, sounding more like a celebrity than an officer of the law. "Officer Taylor, get these people out of here."

Following orders, Officer Taylor headed straight to the reporter, who was a member of his high school graduating class. "Sonja Ashby," he told her, "you need to leave the area."

She put the microphone down and asked, "Is this a murder? Is this related to Mr. Newman's death?"

"I don't know. I just got here. There is no autopsy report yet on Mr. Newman. You need to do as I say and leave the area."

"Kerry?"

"Yes, Sonja?"

"I should have never let you get away," the reporter said as she reached for his hand, massaging it gently and then sashaying her way across the parking lot.

Kerry went over to examine the bodies of Mr. and Mrs. Poulardi. As he knelt down by the couple, he wondered whether either one was saved.

"Officer Taylor," a voice said, making him jump. "You all right?"

"Yes. Good evening, Doctor," said Kerry, standing up to shake hands with the coroner. "It's been a bust day for you."

Doctor Maxwell did not respond but moved in for a closer look at Mrs. Poulardi. "Is your sister here, Officer Taylor?"

Terri replied, "I'm right here, Doctor. I don't have my kit."

"I have mine. Let's check for body fluids."

CHAPTER 21

etective Smadja was about to check the restaurant for any possible witnesses when a clearly irritated Detective Donald O'Connor came charging at him. "Who gave you the authority to release the autopsy report to civilians?" he asked. "I will be personally bringing you up on charges. Son, I am going to have your badge and weapon! Do you have any idea how many codes of ethics you broke? Not only that, but you disobeyed my orders."

Once Detective Smadja felt the tirade was over, he said very calmly, "Detective, first of all, I did not give anyone, civilian or otherwise, the results of Mr. Newman's autopsy. Second, you did not give me any order to report the autopsy findings to you, and third, you are not my authority. I do not answer to you; I answer to the chief. If you have a problem with the autopsy report being shared with a civilian, you need to speak with the chief coroner. And Detective, you need to know that Mr. Newman was murdered."

Detective O'Connor laughed. "According to Strickland, the midget coroner said Newman died of natural causes."

"You'd better check with the doctor before you laugh him off," warned Detective Smadja. "We not only have Mr. Newman's murder, but we are certain about three other unsolved murders."

"And who might they be?"

Detective Smadja hesitated before saying anything, because he did not want another tirade from O'Connor. Also, by bringing up the other murders, he was pointing at holes in O'Connor's investigation that he wanted to first discuss with the chief of police. "They would be Wanda Hall, Mrs. Parker, and City Manager Carter Michaels."

To his surprise, there was no outburst, no sarcasm, no laughter. All Detective O'Connor did was tell the younger man to check with the parking lot attendant to see whether he saw or heard anything, and to submit his report to the chief. He then walked into the restaurant and headed over to where Ronnie and Rod were seated.

Rod said to him, "Detective, what do you know about Angerona?"

CHAPTER 22

Terri Taylor had just attempted to remove natural cavity fluids from the bodies of Mr. and Mrs. Poulardi. This was done with the use of an instrument that would pierce open cavities and extract fluid. She looked at the chief coroner and said, "There is no bodily fluid in either body."

Dr. Maxwell turned to the EMT who had arrived to take the bodies to the morgue. "You can take the bodies."

"Doctor, you need to talk to my brother," Terri said.

"About what?"

"Kerry said he spoke with this couple's daughter tonight on his lunch break."

"He what? She's been dead for twenty-four years!"

"Doctor, you should talk to my brother," Terri repeated.

"Where is he?"

Officer Taylor was at the entrance to the parking lot, explaining to the patrons that they could not get their automobiles until the bodies were removed. One person offered him three hundred dollars to let him leave, which was met with a strong warning that an arrest would follow if that offer was presented again.

The offer made Officer Taylor think there must be some sinister reason behind this guy wanting to leave so desperately. It was also interesting to him that when the television camera crew panned the crowd for the 11:00 p.m. newscast, the man made sure he stayed out of the camera shot. Making a mental note of the man's features and suspicious behavior, Officer Taylor decided that he would later search for the stranger's face among the police blotters. Right now, he was interested in learning more about Darlene Poulardi. Officer Lee said she had been dead for over twenty years. This would be something else he would have to investigate.

"Officer!" the impatient man yelled. "The ambulance is leaving. Can we get our vehicles now?"

"One second. Let me check with the coroner."

Dr. Maxwell was with Terri when Officer Taylor found him. He had seen the officer walking in his direction. "Tell me about your meeting with Darlene Poulardi," he said to the young man, causing Officer Taylor to delay his question of whether the people could move their vehicles.

Kerry looked at his sister, and then back at the doctor.

"I believe you saw her," said the coroner. "And because you saw her, you are in danger."

"I think I can handle myself against a seventeen-year-old girl."

"Officer, she is not seventeen, and she is not a girl. She is an evil being, a pawn of a fallen angel Angerona."

"What?" Kerry asked, surprised. "Terri, is this some kind of religious trick to scare me into accepting Christ? Doctor, what I need to know right now, so I can do my job, is whether these folks can get their vehicles."

"Kerry," Terri said.

"Drop it, sis. Doctor?"

"Yes, the area is clear."

Officer Taylor summoned the patrons into the parking lot to get their vehicles and then called on the parking lot attendants to direct the flow of outgoing traffic. At the same time, the coroner followed the officer, hoping to hear more about this meeting between him and the dead Poulardi girl. No sooner had he started to speak, however, than Kerry cut him off.

"Dr. Maxwell!" Officer Taylor said in his most authoritative police voice. "I am trying to do my job right now. I need you and my sister to leave this area at once."

"Kerry," Terri tried again.

"Now!" Kerry said with a mixture of authority, anger, and what he felt was betrayal from his sister. He thought how nice it would have been to be able to tell his sister that he loved her, and that he wished he would have accepted Jesus Christ as his savior.

CHAPTER 23

Rod and Dobie returned to Conley's Restaurant. They sat back down with Ronnie and Don.

"Dobie, why the great interest in Angerona?" Rod asked.

"Well, Strickland, according to Detective Smadja and the chief coroner, Angerona caused the deaths of four people in Rachael's Point. I need a lead. I need something to go on to catch and question this person."

"Dobie," Rod started, "I think you, Ronnie, and Don know who Angerona is. However, to save time, Angerona is a fallen angel that has the power to grant eternal life. She makes a pact with young females who want to remain youthful. She appeals to their vanity. They make a pact, and in exchange for the bodily fluids, which are given and retained by Angerona from their victims as a sacrifice, they receive the gift of staying young. The followers are dead but do not age."

"So I am looking for a fallen angel?"

"No, Dobie," Rod said. "You are looking for the young, beautiful female who made the pact with Angerona."

Ronnie wanted to know how long this killing spree would last. Rod responded that he did not know, but he believed that someone had made a pact with Angerona, and that person had been here in the past and was in Rachael's Point now. She was responsible for all the deaths that had occurred since Rod had been in town.

Detective Smadja came in the restaurant and walked over to the table where the Four were sitting. "May I speak with you privately, Detective?"

"No," Dobie said. "They can hear what you have to say to me."

"Doctor Maxwell advised me that his preliminary examination of the bodies show that they are void of any fluids in the body cavities, and he believes that all four were murdered."

"Thank you. You can leave. Please go back to the precinct and tell Officer Lee that you will help him transport our newest prisoner, and possible murderer, to county tonight."

"Murderer?"

"Officers Lee and Taylor will fill you in on the charges."

With a perplexed look on his face, Detective Smadja turned and walked out of Conley's Restaurant.

As the detective was leaving, Rod asked, "You think Amy is a murderer?"

"I don't know, Strickland. I do know she was trespassing at the convention center, and I know since you've both been here, three people died. The coroner says they were murdered. Now, I don't believe you are capable of murder. It is Amy with no last name that I am concerned about. I have to go. I suggest all of you go straight home now."

"Dobie," Rod said as he stood up, "I would like to see Amy and speak with her."

"Sorry, Strickland. Visiting hours are over. You will have to visit her in the county lock-up tomorrow." Dobie had that *I am in charge* tone in his voice that Rod could not stand.

"By the way, guys," Rod said. "Whoever Angerona makes the pact with, she returns every eight years to kill and to take the victim's body fluid to Angerona. In the third cycle, or every twenty-four years, the female must return to kill and take the bodily fluid of whoever wronged her. This is the twenty-fourth anniversary of Darlene's death or disappearance. I am putting two and two together and coming up with one of us being the next victim."

Dobie, Ronnie, and Don sat back down at the table. Rod asked them again, "What happened when I left?"

Dobie began, "Don and I put on our hoods over our heads and went to where you left Darlene, but when we got there, she was gone."

Don interjected. "We thought you did something to her. Well, at least Dobie did. I thought you put her in the trunk of the GTO, and she suffocated, and you then buried the body."

"Is that why the police came to arrest me?" Rod asked.

"No," Dobie said in a superior tone. "They came because you were the last one seen with her."

"Okay, but where did the charge of murder come from?"

"My father," Dobie replied. "Once we told him what we were planning to do, he felt that because you had no parents to defend you, it would be easier to place blame on you. You had no family, no one to miss you, no one to stand up for you if you were convicted."

Rod couldn't believe what he was hearing. He looked at Ronnie and said firmly but softly, "I thought I did have family—you and your mother."

"You did," said Ronnie, lowering his head and looking away from Rod. He could not look him in the eyes. "The reason the DA dropped the charges and made a deal was because I told Mom what the plan really was, which involved more than taking Darlene's dress. The plan was that after Wanda got me home, I would miraculously get well, take her home, and come back to Benshoff Hill to rescue her from the two hooded guys that took all of her clothes. She would be grateful and would be mine. But when I got back, she was not there, and none of us knew where she was. We honestly thought you had her, until ..."

"Until what, Ronnie?" coaxed Rod.

"Until nothing!" Dobie said.

"There is more to it than that," Rod said, determined to get the answers that he sought. "You can't tell me that you changed the course of my life over a school-boy crush. Do you know how many people died because I went to the military and became the best of the best? Children who, by my hand, became fatherless or motherless, and mothers and fathers who buried their sons and daughters. There has to be more."

"There isn't," said Dobie. "But tell me more about these murders."

Rod shook his head. "These murders were out of your jurisdiction and were too high-level for you to worry about."

"Murder has no jurisdiction, Strickland."

"Neither does cover-up," Rod said as he stood up again. "Ronnie, I will be getting my bag and staying at the hotel."

"That's not necessary," Ronnie said, also standing.

"Yes, it is. I will leave the GTO in the garage."

As Rod was leaving, he passed by Officer Taylor.

Officer Taylor said to Dobie, "Detective, I just got a call from the station. The prisoner is gone."

"Which one, Officer Taylor?"

"The girl, Amy."

Dobie got to his feet, having the feeling that this girl has a connection to Darlene and could impact the plans for Saturday. He looked at Rod and went out of the restaurant.

Rod said to Officer Taylor, "How did she escape?"

"I don't know, sir. Officer Lee said the cell is empty, and she is gone." Officer Taylor looked at his watch. It was 10:04 p.m. He remembered Amy telling him that she would only be in jail for two hours.

Ronnie, Don, and Rod left the restaurant, and Officer Taylor followed. The men went to their vehicles, and Officer Taylor went over to the parking lot attendants. He checked to see if they needed assistance and was told they had everything under control. Officer Taylor went to his cruiser, got in, and called dispatch. "Dispatch, this is Car 32, Officer Taylor. I am on my way to the station, unless there are other orders."

"This is dispatch. You are clear to come in if everything is wrapped up at Conley's."

"I'm on my way." Officer Taylor started his cruiser, and before he put it in drive, he looked in his rearview mirror. In the back seat, he saw Darlene Poulardi. She was the last person he saw. She whispered in his ear, and he slumped over the steering wheel.

Darlene then went on to extract all of Officer Taylor's body fluids. The internal fluids turned to a mist as Darlene collected them. The vial that she was using had a six-inch steel needle attached to the bottom of it, and it easily punctured the skin. Although any part of the victim's body could be easily punctured with this device. Darlene preferred the base of the neck. Once the needle was inserted, it was as if the vial was magnetized. The fluids would be drawn, and as blood turned red once it received oxygen, the fluids that were extracted turned to a mist and filled the vial.

Darlene hid the specimen inside of her duster, along with other vials that contained body fluids belonging to Carter Michaels, Craig Newman, and her parents. She had one more that had to be collected tomorrow—this being the twenty-fourth year and the third cycle of her pact with Angerona.

Darlene stepped outside of the cruiser and slowly glided upward. As she soared unseen over Rachael's Point, she smiled and thought about what a glorious twenty-four years it had been. She remembered the night when she'd met Angerona. Those stupid boys—Don Hart, Ronnie Parker, Rod Strickland, and Dobie O'Connor—had planned to embarrass her, sexually abuse her, and make her some kind of slave to them. She laughed now as she landed on the roof of city hall. If they had known that she had made a pact with Angerona months before, and that she was promised the gift of staying young forever by agreeing that every year, she would bring five vials of bodily fluid from her victims, and every eight years bring the bodily fluid of someone connected to the four boys who had tried to wrong her, they would have chosen someone else to try and humiliate.

This was the third cycle and the twenty-fourth year. Darlene needed to bring Angerona body fluids from one of the four boys who had tried to attack her. When she returned to Rachael's Point, she decided to let them make a choice, remembering how she had revealed herself to Dobie as he was coming out of the Franklin Street Lounge. It was about 2:00 a.m., and she had called out his name as he was getting into his car. He had turned and looked at her but did not recognize her.

"Dobie O'Connor, I am surprised that you don't remember me."

Then something clicked in Dobie, and he realized who was speaking to him. Frightened, he leaned against the car, unable to speak.

"Dobie," Darlene remembered saying, "it's me, Darlene. And to answer your question, I have not aged."

"How can that be?"

"Your finite mind would never understand. I am here to collect a debt that is owed to my benefactor."

"What debt? We did nothing to you!" Dobie said, his voice shaking.

As she walked to the edge of the roof, she looked out over the miserable city. She thought about the fear on Dobie's face six months ago when she'd told him, "The debt you and your friends owe is for your failed, miserable attempt to humiliate me. Look at me. I am young and will stay alive forever. I have killed four people, and on the anniversary of the day you took me to Benshoff Hill Cemetery, I will kill you or one of your friends. Do you want to die and then lose all of your bodily fluids? Or do you want to spare yourself by helping me?"

The door leading to the roof opened, and Darlene was jolted back to the present. As she watched Dobie coming toward her, she decided that he should be the one to die. Six months ago, he had quickly given up the city manager. Now here he was again, ready to sacrifice his friend Rod Strickland, the angel lecturer.

"Darlene," said Dobie, "I just received a report that you spoke to one of my officers."

"Don't worry about him," Darlene said.

"Well, I have to. Officer Taylor told another officer and an official from the coroner's office that he saw you."

"Dobie," she said as if she were talking to a child, "don't worry about it. What I need to know is where Rod Strickland will be at 7:30 p.m. tomorrow."

Dobie assured her that Rod would be backstage at the convention center, alone in a dressing room. "There will be a security guard in the wings of the stage, and one at the back entrance who will be called away by me at seven."

"Sounds like a plan," Darlene said from where she stood on the edge of the roof. "By the way, you will be getting a call telling you that Officer Taylor has been found dead. I think he died of natural causes." She laughed. "Four vials, and one to go." With that, she walked off the roof and into the night air.

Though the night was chilly, Dobie had sweated through his shirt and jacket. He was terrified and walked around the roof trying to collect his thoughts. *One more day, and this nightmare will be over for at least the next twenty-four years. I have to think. Officer Taylor is dead. There will be no way of stopping the coroner from making a case that there is a serial killer on the loose.*

Dobie decided he would have to go to the coroner and buy into the story of a serial killer who had escaped tonight. Even better, he needed to go to the media. *What was that reporter's name? Something silly. Oh, yeah—Sonja Ashby.* He was no longer sweating. He had a plan.

He got down from the roof of city hall, confident that this would all be over tomorrow night, with the headlines declaring the sensational death of world-famous lecturer Rod Strickland. The official cause would be murder by a deranged follower. Amy with no last name was in custody, but due to inadequate facilities at the city lock-up, she had escaped. Upon her escape, she'd murdered Officer Taylor.

When he got downstairs, Dobie started giving orders. "Has Officer Taylor arrived?"

"No," was Officer Lee's reply.

"Take a squad car and find him!"

"Yes, sir."

Dobie walked over to Detective Smadja. "John, you are working late," he observed.

"I normally do."

"John, I am sorry about my actions tonight, but there have been three deaths today, and I was on edge," Dobie said in a civil voice.

"No problem," replied Smadja.

Dobie turned to leave but walked back over to the detective. "John?"

"Yes, Detective O'Connor?"

"I am calling WCNE. I'm going to make a statement about these murders."

"Don't you think you should run this by the chief?"

Dobie reached out and placed his hand on Detective Smadja's shoulder. "I don't want to disturb him, but you are free to call him."

CHAPTER 24

Sonja Ashby, whose real name was Ashley Smith, was sitting at her desk. It was fifteen minutes before the start of the eleven o'clock news, and twenty-seven minutes before she had to report on the deaths of Mr. and Mrs. Poulardi. She had nothing. She had that appearance of Darlene Poulardi, who'd vanished twenty-four years ago on her prom night, but as far as her parents being found dead in Conley's parking lot, the police would make no comment on the cause of death. She only had video of the people who were standing around the parking lot. It would be good if she could get Kerri to give her something. She would gladly accept off-the-record statements.

Just then her phone rang. "Hello? Yes, this is Sonja. What? You will go on camera? Detective O'Connor, I will be right there." She hung up and then yelled to her producer, "Hooray! I have a story on the three deaths that happened today, and possibly a fourth."

"We're on in four minutes!" her producer protested.

"I will do my story live from city hall. Bump me down to 11:20 for a live feed. Kenny! she screamed. "Truck still set up for the live feed we were going to do from the parking lot?"

"Yeah."

"Great. Let's roll—now!"

Kenny lost no time in following Sonja's instructions, but not so much because she was his superior. It was because he had secretly been in love with her since fifth grade geography, when they'd teamed up together on mapping ancient Mongolia. He realized that he had no chance with her, but the fact that he was working with her was good enough for him.

He opened the door for Sonja. She got in, and he closed the door and went around to the driver's side. To him, she was the most beautiful black woman he had seen in his life, with shoulder-length black hair, bronze skin that was always aglow, and full, kissable lips.

"Kenny!" He was snapped out of his fantasy world by the authoritative voice behind those full lips. "Let's roll!" Sonja ordered.

Kenny started the truck and pulled out of the WCNE parking lot.

CHAPTER 25

Rod pulled the GTO into the Parkers' driveway behind Ronnie's SUV. He pressed the garage door opener, and when the door went up, he pulled the car into the left side of the garage. He got out, walked out of the garage, and found Ronnie waiting for him by the front door.

"Rod, please don't leave," Ronnie said. "What happened twenty-four years ago ... I was seventeen, and I was scared and under pressure."

Rod kept walking. He put his hand on the doorknob and turned to face Ronnie, "What other pressures are you under? I know that there is more to me coming home than just a lecture. Why do you want me back here?"

Ronnie was terrified. The look on his face said more than any words could have.

Rod placed his hand on Ronnie's shoulder, looked him in the eye, and said, "You, Don, and Dobie wanted me here to be part of the twenty-fourth anniversary of Darlene's Poulardi's disappearance. Why?"

Ronnie was unable to respond. He stared past Rod into the doorway of the house. The door opened from the inside, and standing in the doorway of his home was this woman with short brown hair wearing a long duster. He knew without any introduction that this was Amy with no last name. "Good evening," Rod said to the woman with a sigh of relief followed by a smile.

* * *

Officer Dobie O'Connor was set for his press conference with WCNE and the reporters from the *Rachael's Point Ledger*. "As you know," he began, "there have been three deaths in our city, and a possible fourth that we are trying to substantiate. We have determined that the cause of death of Mr. Craig Newman, Mr. Darryl Poulardi, and Mrs. Antoinette Poulardi was a result of murder. We identified a suspect and took her into custody this afternoon, but she escaped approximately one hour ago while we were preparing to transport her to county lock-up. Now I will take your questions."

"Detective O'Connor, Sonja Ashby of WCNE TV. We are live. Do you have any idea where the suspect is at this time, and can you give us a name and description?"

"We have her first name only. Her name is Amy. She is five feet six inches, is approximately 130 pounds with an athletic build, and has short brown hair. She will probably be wearing a long, black duster. We consider her armed and dangerous."

"Armed and dangerous, Detective? How did the victims die?"

"Based upon what we have from the coroner, all of the bodily fluids were extracted from the victims."

"What? Detective, are you saying that we have a killer that is stealing fluid from the victims' bodies?" The reporter from the *Ledger* asked.

Sonja glared at the reporter. This was her interview. "Detective, I was at the murder scene at Conley's parking lot, and there was no sign of a struggle and no blood stains. So how is this suspect Amy removing all the body fluids?"

"We don't know, Sonja. We are early in the investigation. We will be working closely with the coroner's office. I have time for one more question."

"Detective, you said that there was maybe a fourth murder. Who is the fourth victim?"

"Sonja, you know I can't reveal that until the next of kin have been notified. Thank you. I have to leave." With that, Detective O'Connor left the room.

Sonja turned to the camera and said, "Trey, as you have heard from Detective Donald O'Connor, we have had three confirmed murders today, and a possible fourth murder. All of the victims were drained of their bodily fluids. We will stay on top of this story as it develops. This is Sonja Ashby, live at the Rachael's Point Police Department."

"Sonja, the police indicated that there were no body fluids to be found in any of the victims. Do they know if the suspect has any ties to a cult?"

What a stupid question, Sonja thought. Detective O'Connor had already said that they had a suspect in custody who'd escaped. If there was a cult connection, he would have mentioned it.

Widening her smile so as not to show her irritation, she told the news anchor that there did not appear to be any connection with a cult at this time, but that she would report on any new developments as the investigation progressed. The anchor thanked her, and then Sonja turned to Kenny, her cameraman. "Are we clear?"

"Yes," he said, taking the camera off his shoulder.

"What an idiot!" Sonja said.

"I'm sorry, Sonja. Did I miss a shot?" asked Kenny, feeling very hurt.

"No, not you, Kenny," Sonja said, placing her hand on his shoulder. "I was talking about Trey 'Mister 11:00 Anchor Man' Thomas. Wasn't he listening to the interview? That follow-up question was asked to try to embarrass me." She removed her hand from Kenny's shoulder and handed him her microphone.

Kenny began wrapping up Sonja's equipment as she walked toward the exit door.

"Hey, Sonja, what do you make of what O'Connor said?" The question came from Oliver Ross, the *Ledger* reporter who'd tried to interrupt her interview.

"What do you mean, what do I think? We have three confirmed murders and maybe a fourth. I think that we have a psycho on the loose killing people in Rachael's Point."

Oliver Ross smiled. "Sonja, I was here investigating contradicting arrest records based on a tip that there is possible dissension between beat cops and detectives regarding when the suspect … what was her name?"

"Amy," Sonja interjected.

"Yeah," Oliver continued, "when Amy was arrested. I was here from late afternoon—say, 5:00 p.m.—and have not left since."

"Look, Oliver, I have to go back to the station to edit and do voice-overs for this piece." Sonja was making the point that her medium of television was more demanding and involved more detail than writing an article and sending it to print.

Oliver ignored Sonja's attempt to make herself feel important. "I was here when Amy was arrested," he said. "I was here when the call came in regarding the deaths of the Poulardi's. Here is the scoop: Amy was still in lock-up."

"What?" Sonja cried, moving closer to Oliver Ross.

"Amy was still in the lock-up. Here is another tidbit for your editing and voice-overs. Kerri Taylor told his sister and Officer Calvin Lee that earlier tonight he spoke with Poulardi's daughter on the roof—the same girl who's been missing for twenty-four years."

Sonja could not believe her ears. "Why didn't you say something while we were on the air?"

Oliver, who stood at least three inches taller than Sonja, leaned forward, placed both of his hands on her shoulders, kissed her on the cheek, looked her in the eye, and said with a smile, "Darling, this was *your* interview."

CHAPTER 26

Amy, Ronnie, and Rod were in the living room. It was large at twelve feet by fourteen feet, with wood flooring. There was an oak table in front of the couch where Ronnie was sitting and two matching end tables. The room had no ceiling lights, but in opposite corners of the room, there were two lamp stands. Ronnie noticed that the lamps cast a street light effect on Rod's face as he stood in the entryway of the room. He also could see beads of sweat on his face.

"Tell me, Ronnie" said Amy, moving away from the huge LED television that was in front of the bay window and now standing at Rod's side, "what you know about Angerona and her emissary? And when and where are you going to attack Rod?"

Ronnie was emphatic. "I have no idea who Angerona is. Neither do I know anything about an emissary."

"Why did you invite me back to Rachael's Point?" Rod asked Ronnie.

There was a long silence, and then Ronnie said two words. "To die."

Rod felt a rush of anger that would have showed on his face if it had not been for his black-ops training, which taught him to show no reaction on his face in any situation unless it was for the benefit of the mission.

Amy walked around the coffee table, sat down on the sofa beside Ronnie, and said, "Ronnie, I saw Mr. Newman die. I am sure you know that the three murders were done by the same person."

"Three deaths?" Ronnie and Rod said at the same time.

"Yes. Officer Kerry Taylor was murdered the same way the Poulardis were murdered. I need to know who the murderer is, Ronnie. I need a name."

Rod looked at Ronnie. "Is it possible? Ronnie, is it Darlene?"

* * *

Downtown, Sonja and Kenny walked out of city hall. Her mind was working overtime. She needed to find Officer Taylor and get his story on his conversation with Darlene Poulardi. Where had she been for twenty-four years? Was she aware of the death of her parents? Why was she on the roof of city hall?

As they reached the television truck, she made the decision to not call her producer. She would get the story first and then interrupt regular programming. She would have it as breaking news in the middle of *The Tonight Show.*

"Kenny, I am about to make a name for myself. Remember when we were in fifth grade and had to do the map of Mongolia?"

"Yes," he said.

"Well, we are teaming up again to chart unknown territory."

Kenny looked at her and thought she must be losing it, but he would never say it to her. Instead, he asked, "Back to the studio?"

"No," Sonja said, "let's ride up and down the streets of Rachael's Point. We need to find Officer Taylor. Let's start by going to his house, and then to Conley's."

Kenny pulled the WCNE truck out of the parking lot and made a left turn onto Main Street. They crossed over Washington and then Monroe. As they crossed Franklin, Sonja yelled, "Stop! Kenny, back up!" Fortunately, there were no cars behind them. Kenny slammed his foot hard on the brake, causing equipment to slide forward from the bed of the truck and striking the back of the front seats.

"Kenny," Sonja said, looking at her co-worker, "are you trying to kill us? Back up to the two police cruisers on the corner."

Kenny backed up, crossed over Franklin, and turned down the street. As they got closer, they could see Officer Calvin Lee with his left hand on top of his police car and his right hand holding his stomach, looking like he was ill. He didn't hear the truck pull up, and neither did he see Sonja and Kenny with the camera and microphone coming toward him. Sonja signaled to Kenny, and he turned on the camera.

"Officer Lee, Sonja Ashby of WCNE. Could you tell me what is happening here? It is our understanding that the bodies that were found here tonight were that of murder victims. Detective O'Connor told us that there was a fourth. Have you found the fourth body?"

Officer Lee said nothing. He opened the door of his cruiser, picked up the radio, and called the dispatch. "Dispatch, this is Officer Lee, I need to speak with Detective O'Connor, and we also need the coroner back out at Conley's."

With microphone and camera still at the ready, Sonja resumed questioning Officer Lee as soon as he ended his call. "Officer Lee, who is the fourth victim?" she persisted.

The officer pointed to the parked police car.

"What does the police car have to do with the fourth victim?" asked Sonja.

Before the officer could answer, Dobie's voice came over the radio. "Lee, what did you find?"

"Officer Taylor, sir. Officer Taylor is dead."

"I am on my way. Secure the scene."

Sonja moved away from Officer Lee as he got out of the car. Her mind was racing. Kerry Taylor, dead? That couldn't be possible. She had spoken to him less than an hour ago.

Meanwhile, Kenny took advantage of the opportunity to get as many pictures as possible of a dead Officer Taylor still in his car. He was about to take another shot when he heard a clicking sound behind him.

"If you do not put your camera down and move away from my partner's vehicle, I will kill you!" Overcome with emotion at the death of his fellow officer and what he felt was his body being disrespected, Officer Lee had drawn his weapon, pulled the hammer back, and was ready to rectify what he felt was a show of dishonor for the memory of his partner.

Sonja looked at Officer Lee and could tell that he was not going to repeat himself. "Kenny, turn off the camera and put all of the equipment in the truck," she said. "We are leaving."

"But Sonja, the story—"

"Kenny, don't become the story. Just do what I said!"

Kenny turned off the camera. He glared at Officer Lee to show him that he was not afraid, and he began wrapping up the equipment

Sonja spoke softly to Officer Lee, who kept his weapon pointed at Kenny. "Officer, has anyone contacted Mrs. Taylor?"

Calvin Lee, officer of the Rachael's Point Police Department and the partner of the now deceased Kerry Taylor, lowered his weapon and began to cry. Sonja put her arms around him and cried with him for the death of a good man.

CHAPTER 27

Ronnie finished telling Amy and Rod again about what had happened at Benshoff Hill Cemetery. He explained how Darlene came back. "Two nights after the prom, I got a call from Dobie. He needed to meet me and Don at his house. When we got there he was scared—and Rod, you know Dobie would never show fear. He said that Darlene had returned.

"This was good news, we thought, until Dobie told us what we were required to do if we wanted to stay alive. He said that Darlene had a pact with a demon or fallen angel, or maybe the devil himself. This fallen angel wanted the bodily fluids of people who were connected to us."

"Connected to you how? And why their body fluids?" asked Rod.

"We didn't ask, and at that point it didn't matter," Ronnie continued. "Regardless of the connection, she wanted the fluids. The agreement was for Darlene to return to Rachael's Point every eight years for the purpose of collecting these fluids. And in the twenty-fourth year, she would come back for one of us.

"Don and I thought it was a joke, but Dobie assured us that this was no joke and to prove it. Darlene took a life that night. She killed Mr. Condo, the high school principal."

"Ronnie, why wasn't I a part of this meeting?" Rod asked.

"Because Darlene did not want anyone to know that she was alive."

"Have you seen Darlene since the disappearance?" Amy wanted to know.

"No," Ronnie replied.

"Has anyone other than Mr. O'Connor seen her?" Amy asked.

"No, not to my knowledge."

"So you are just taking the word of Mr. O'Connor that Darlene is coming for Rod."

Ronnie didn't answer immediately. He waited more than a few seconds before saying, "A lot of planning went into getting Rod here and getting him booked at the convention center."

"Including the death of Carter Michaels," Rod said.

"Yes," Ronnie replied.

"What's the plan?" Amy asked. "Where and when is Darlene supposed to extract Rod's body fluids?"

"Tomorrow, before the lecture. I need to have Rod there at 6:00 p.m." Ronnie turned to look at Rod. "Sometime before you are introduced, Darlene will visit with you."

"Rod," Amy said, "is your lecture ready?"

"Yes, it is."

"Good. I am looking forward to hearing you."

"What about Darlene?" Ronnie asked.

Amy started walking toward the door. "I will handle Darlene," she said. "Stay here, and neither of you leave this house until it is time to go to the convention center tomorrow. Rod, you will need the full armor of God tonight and tomorrow. Call Dr. Leventry and Pastor Kimble, and have them pray for you and for the success of your lecture."

She looked at Ronnie. "Don't tell anyone that you saw or spoke to me unless they ask. I would not want you to lie. Remember, our battle is not against flesh and blood, but principalities. The only way we will win this battle and be delivered from the curse is by the word of God."

Ronnie stood up from the couch as Amy walked out of the door. He started to follow her, but Rod grabbed his arm. "She won't be there," he told his friend. Ronnie went out of the door anyway and did not find Amy. He looked at Rod, who shrugged. "I told you."

"Rod, are you going to talk?"

"There is really nothing to say, Ronnie. You have said and done it all. I am going to call Dr. Leventry and my pastor. I suggest that you repent and ask Jesus into your life. He will forgive you, restore you, and deliver you from all unrighteousness."

Ronnie felt tears coming to his eyes "But what about you? Rod, will you forgive me?"

"Already done," Rod answered.

Ronnie could not handle any more. He fell to his knees right where he stood and said, "God, I am sorry for all I have done. Rod said, and I have read, that Jesus died so I could have eternal life. I know Jesus died, and I believe that you raised him from the dead, and that he is with you right now. Please save me. Please deliver me from evil. I accept you right now and will proclaim it and you wherever I go."

The last few words that Ronnie spoke were unintelligible. Overshadowed by the Holy Spirit, he had spoken in an unknown language, like the people in the Book of Acts on the Day of Pentecost.

Rod was overjoyed at Ronnie's conversion. He cried and praised God right along with Ronnie. Several hours later, the two were still talking about the goodness and power of God. Rod opened up the word of God to Ronnie, who received it like a sponge. They rejoiced because salvation had come to the Parker house, where they'd grown to love each other like brothers.

CHAPTER 28

D r. Maxwell, Detective O'Connor, Officer Lee, Sonja Ashby, Kenny, and two EMTs were at the murder scene. They had all been at murder scenes before. There was normally the splattered blood pattern, the gruesome twist of the body, and the smell of blood that was like copper. However, other than Mrs. Poulardi lying on her face, the scene was peaceful and almost organized, as if they were murdered by a friend.

"Detective, we have another murder by 'natural causes,'" Dr. Maxwell said.

"And how were the body fluids removed?" Sonja asked hastily.

Dobie jumped in and with a wave of his right hand told everyone present, "We are making no official comments at this time."

"Detective, the cameras are off," Sonja pointed out. "I'm not here as a reporter. Kerry was a personal friend of mine. I would like to give comfort to his wife when I speak to her."

"We will handle that, Sonja," Dobie said dismissively.

"Okay," Sonja said in response. "Kenny, get the camera, call the station, and let them know that we will need to interrupt programming for a live feed."

"Can't that report wait until morning?" Dobie asked.

"Sure, if I have something to report, Dobie." Sonja knew using the detective's nickname would make him angry, because she was not a member of the "just call me Dobie" club.

Dobie grabbed her arm at the bicep and squeezed. "What did you call me?"

In a flash, Kenny ran toward him.

"Come on, camera boy!" taunted Dobie.

Dr. Maxwell yelled, "Stop! Detective, take your hands off Ms. Ashby immediately." He then pointed at Kenny. "Young man, you really don't want to attack a police officer who has a loaded weapon to protect him, do you?"

The EMTs looked at each other, both men having the same thought: *The littlest person out here commands the most authority.*

Dobie let go of Sonja's arm, and Kenny backed down, realizing that Dr. Maxwell had saved him from getting a severe beating.

"Right now, Ms. Ashby," said the coroner, "we don't know how or, probably more important, why fluids are being taken from the bodies. Please, when you report this, let the viewers know that there is no vampirism. The blood remains in the body, but all other fluids are removed like a mortician would do when he is getting ready for the embalming process."

"May I quote you on that, Dr. Maxwell?"

"Certainly. As a matter of fact, I have some theories. Mind you, they are only theories of who is behind the killings."

"Wait a minute, Bernie!" Dobie exclaimed.

"Dobie," Sonja said in a sweet, childlike voice, "may I speak to you privately?" She walked away from the chief coroner and Kenny, who were both amazed that after what had just happened, she again called him Dobie. Surprisingly, Dobie walked away with Sonja.

One of the EMTs said to no one in particular, "If looks could kill, the chief would be examining another body."

"Dobie," Sonja began, but she was interrupted by the detective.

"The next time you call me Dobie Ms. Ashby, please know that it will be the last time," he said through gritted teeth. "You will not be able to show your face on WCNE."

"Is that a threat, Detective O'Connor?" she said, smiling.

"No, it is a promise that an escaped prisoner will find you and disfigure you for life, and then he'll escape Rachael's Point without being apprehended. Now, what do you want?"

Detective O'Connor said this with such coldness that Sonja felt a chill run down her spine. She decided not to challenge him on what she had found out about Amy: that she was not the one who had murdered the Poulardis. Instead, she said, "Detective O'Connor, I really need a follow-up to your news conference tonight. I am sure Dr. Maxwell's theories are out there, but I need something as a follow-up story."

Dobie smiled, satisfied that he had made his point about her respecting him and not calling him by his nickname. "Just don't make me or the police department look bad. Also, you might want to speak with Rod Strickland."

"The gentleman who is here to do the lecture on angels?" Sonja asked.

"Yes. There appears to be some connection between our suspect and him."

"Where is he staying?" Sonja now was in full reporter mode.

"I can't give you that information, but he will be at the convention center tomorrow at 6:00 p.m. I will make sure your press pass allows you to have access to him."

"Great! Thanks, Dob—" Sonja caught herself. "Detective O'Connor." She turned to Kenny. "We are done here. Dr. Maxwell, when can we meet at your office?"

"Give me an hour, and let's meet at the coffee house."

"See you there." Sonja was very pleased with how this was going to turn out. Dr. Maxwell's theories on four deaths, speaking with famed lecturer Rod Strickland regarding his connection with the suspect in two of the four murders, and the fact that Rod Strickland was childhood friends with Dobie.

Yeah, Dobie. What an idiot! Sonja thought. She had him on record threatening her life. She now pulled the MP3 player from under her blouse. Detective O'Connor had no clue that every word of their conversation was being recorded.

She looked over at Kenny. "Thank you for wanting to come to my aid when Dobie grabbed my arm. However, I cannot take you to CNN with me."

Kenny started the truck. "What?"

"Oh, nothing," Sonja said, and began daydreaming of her anchor seat.

Dobie watched as the WCNE truck left the scene. He smiled and thought, *Sonja Ashby, real name Ashley Smith. You will die along with Rod tomorrow. I am sure Darlene will have no problem with you being there.*

Then you will have personal knowledge of how she removes the fluid from the body—you'll simply never be able to report it.

"Bernie, are you almost done?" Dobie asked.

"I am done, Detective. I will see you in the morning."

"I need the cause of death by 10:00 a.m."

"I told you the cause of death."

"Fine. Just put it in writing," Dobie said, thinking to himself that the little munchkin of a coroner deserved to die too.

CHAPTER 29

The moon was high over the Benshoff Hill Cemetery, making even the lowest headstone visible. There was dew on the grass, and unlike in the horror movies, there was no fog. Neither were there any hooting owls, or any sounds of other animals in the entire cemetery.

Standing at the east end of the cemetery, however, was a lone figure. Darlene Poulardi, now neither human nor animal, but an ungodly, unfeeling entity that used to be a young teenage girl. Now she was this thing that had made a pact with the fallen angel Angerona twenty-four years ago.

Angerona was beautiful. She looked like she was thirty years old. She had dark hair and dark, penetrating eyes. Her skin tone was perfect, not pasty white but like smooth, milky white chocolate. She had no wings and stood five feet five inches tall. She wore blue jeans and a buttoned-down, aqua-colored shirt. On her feet were black boots. Her dark hair flowed over the black duster she was wearing.

Twenty-four years ago was the night she'd explained the pact of never-ending life and the promise of growing no older to Darlene Poulardi. The agreement was immediately ratified with the taking of all bodily fluids from Darlene's body. After Angerona had extracted the body fluids without Darlene dying, Angerona had given her the secret words that she would whisper in her victims' ears, bringing on a sudden death that would seem to be caused by a massive heart attack. Darlene would then have up to three minutes to collect all of the person's bodily fluids.

Angerona wanted no blood. She had made it clear that any blood collected would make the pact null and void, and Darlene would immediately return to her chronological age at a speed that would take her life in an instant.

Now, as Darlene stood alone on the opposite end of the cemetery, she did not regret having made the pact. She did not regret having her folks go through the agony of thinking she was dead. After all, they did receive money to shut up and leave town.

She'd enjoyed scaring Dobie the night she'd appeared to him. She had wanted to kill him, but she knew he would become her ally over the next twenty-four years. So far, he had followed the instructions she had given him. As a boy, he was truly despicable. Now as a man, he was even more so. He had handled the five murders that she had committed well. She absentmindedly looked at the vials of fluid that were inside the special pocket of her black duster. There was one more vial to go, and she had Dobie to thank for setting up that next encounter. She had actually come back for him, but he'd convinced her that a better candidate would be the noted lecturer and lover of Jesus Christ, Rod Strickland.

Darlene remembered that Rod Strickland was the only one on the night of the prom who was willing to help her. He was one of the four boys who wanted to humiliate her, but he wasn't going to take part in the removal of her clothes and the taking of pictures of her naked body. At least, that was what Dobie had told her about Rod when he thought he was going to be her first victim. Dobie must have thought that Darlene had the power to tell if he was lying or telling the truth, which she did not have. Or maybe it was the fear that was inside of him. Whatever it was, he was truthful.

She would not feel guilty about killing Rod and taking his fluids, because he was a Christian. Angerona had never said so, but it was obvious to Darlene that the goddess was pleased when fluid from the body of a Christian was brought to her. It had something to do with the time she was being worshipped as a Roman goddess and the Christians had refused to bow to her. *So, Rod's death is a plus,* Darlene concluded. She would have to wait eight more years for Dobie, though she made him think his number would not be up for another twenty-four years. *It will be twenty-four years for Ronnie Parker or Don Hart, but not for Dobie O'Connor Jr., the coward. No, not for the coward.*

CHAPTER 30

Rod had not slept. This was not unusual for him; he normally prayed the night before a lecture and fasted the day before. After the lecture, he would treat himself to a meal that included a medium-well steak, a huge baked potato with sour cream and butter, and a side of broccoli. He would then drink an Arnold Palmer.

Last night, he prayed with Ronnie after his friend had accepted Jesus Christ as savior. They had talked until 5:00 a.m. about God's love and grace.

After Ronnie went to bed, Rod called Dr. Leventry and told him everything, including what he believed about Amy—that she was an angel from God. When Dr. Leventry disagreed, Rod thought it best not to argue; they could debate the issue another time. The conversation ended with Dr. Leventry praying for his protégé, reminding him that no weapons formed against him would prosper because he loved the Lord and was called according to his purpose. "Rod," Dr. Leventry said, "put on the full armor of God."

Next, Rod called Pastor Kimble, who was finishing breakfast. They also prayed together. Rod did not go into detail with Pastor Kimble as to what was happening. He only told him that his life was in danger. Like Amy and Dr. Leventry, Pastor Kimble encouraged him to put on the full armor of God.

Rod wanted to go downtown, walk around, observe the people, and pray. That was what he normally did before giving a lecture. He wanted to know the spirit of the city.

"Ronnie!" he called as he walked down the hall to Ronnie's room. There was no answer from Ronnie.

Downstairs, Rod found a note on the coffee table. The single sentence read, "I am going to end this now."

"Oh, no!" Rod gasped. He ran upstairs, grabbed the shirt that he had thrown over the bed, ran out of the house, and got into the GTO. He thought that he would likely find Ronnie in Dobie's office. Rod pulled out of the driveway and started down Menoher Boulevard. As he came around the curve at the bottom of the hill, he came upon a long line of vehicles. He thought there must be an accident of some kind, because he could see an ambulance, a police officer directing traffic, a WCNE van, and a news reporter. He stepped out of the GTO to see what had happened.

"Rod."

He heard the voice that had come from the direction of the ambulance. "What happened?" he asked, recognizing Don Hart. "What happened, Don?"

Don placed his hand on Rod's shoulder, "It's Ronnie."

At the start of the wailing of the ambulance siren, they both looked up and watched as the vehicle left for the hospital.

"Come with me," Don said.

"No. The GTO is over here. I will do a U-turn, and we will be at the hospital before they arrive."

"Let's roll," Don said.

* * *

Sonja could not believe all of this was happening. She had just gotten approval from her producer and the station head to go with the story. The fact that Detective O'Connor had lied about the suspect he had in custody and the fact that this person murdered the Poulardis would be a story that may go national.

She got permission to air Dr. Maxwell's theory that there was a cult at work who worshipped the goddess Angerona. The doctor could not figure out how or why fluids were being removed from the bodies, but the story was that he could prove that this practice had started sixteen years ago with the death of Wanda Hall. He also believed that the arrival of angel expert and former Rachael's Point resident Rod Strickland was the catalyst for the deaths of Craig Newman, Darryl and Antoinette Poulardi, and Officer Kerry Taylor, a fine policeman and friend who admitted to having spoken with Darlene Poulardi the night her parents were murdered.

Sonja had already started her research. She had not slept the night before because she was so energized by the story. She began by pulling from the archived photos of Darlene Poulardi. Sonja thought Darlene was a pretty girl, but one with a face that said, "I'm better than you." She had also pulled photos of Rod Strickland. It was interesting that Wanda Hall, who'd died sixteen years ago and was the first to have all of the body fluids removed, was Rod Strickland's date to the prom the night Darlene Poulardi went missing. She wondered whether there was a connection, and she went on to research all of the murders that Dr. Maxwell felt were connected.

All of the victims were listed as having died of natural causes. Though it was never reported, everyone had had all their bodily fluids removed. *If this is a cult,* thought Sonja, *it has must have been around since or before Darlene's death.*

"Oh, my God!" she suddenly burst out. Then caught herself as others looked at her. "Sorry, guys. I had a light bulb moment." She smiled, though no one else returned it. *Could Darlene have been part of the cult, and when she died, the cult decided to avenge her death? But if so, why had they not killed Strickland?* She concluded that it may be because he had spent time in jail and was forced to join the military.

Sonja looked at her watch and realized that she had to speak with Kerry Taylor's wife, to get her reaction to her husband's death. So far this morning, there was no comment from the chief of police other than they were conducting an ongoing investigation into Officer Taylor's death, as well as all of the other deaths that had occurred yesterday. No mention of bodily fluid, no mention of Darlene Poulardi, and no mention of any potential suspects. She picked up her purse and walked over to Lynn Eastwick, the head cameraman. "Ready?"

"Let's roll," he said.

Kenny, who had been editing the footage he had taken the night before, looked up at Sonja who, walked by him without a look or word. Sonja was assigned the station's best cameraman for this assignment. She never gave Kenny a second thought for this assignment. As they walked by, Kenny heard Sonja say, "CNN, here I come.

CHAPTER 31

D on and Rod reached the hospital just as Ronnie was being taken by
stretcher into the ER.

"Park your car there," said Don, pointing at a space marked for doctors only. When the attendant came over to protest, he recognized the city manager and nodded to him, indicating that the car would be fine where it was. Don entered the ER, followed closely by Rod. "Where did they take the patient that just came in?" Don asked the woman at the registration desk.

"He was taken to area A, Mr. Hart, but—"

Don did not wait for the receptionist to protest. He went through the double hospital doors, followed by Rod. They turned right and went to the far corner of a huge room. These screened-off areas were more like cubicles, big enough only for a hospital bed and a night stand. There was a doctor in area A shouting orders above the crowd. As the two men approached the nurse's station, one of the nurses stopped them.

"We are friends of Ronnie Parker," said Don.

"I know who you both are," the nurse said. "You need to go back to the waiting area."

"How is he?" Rod asked.

"Critical," the nurse said rather impatiently.

Don and Rod went back to the waiting area, where they sat in silence for thirty minutes. Eventually Don asked, "I wonder where Ronnie was going?"

No answer came from Rod. He was praying and not paying attention to Don.

"Rod, did he say where he was going?"

"No, he didn't tell me. Listen, can you get a ride back to your office? I need to get ready for tonight."

"Tonight?" Don asked. Then he remembered Rod's speaking engagement, and he quickly added, "Yes, of course. Tonight. Everything is ready, and security will be there at 6:00 p.m. to take you to your dressing room."

"Thank you."

A nurse came into the waiting room. "Rod Strickland?"

"That's me."

"Come with me, please."

Don started to follow them.

"Mr. Hart," the nurse said, "the patient specifically asked for Mr. Strickland."

"Diane, does he know I am out here?"

"He knows." Diane Bell was enjoying this. Don Hart thought that every knee should bow when he was in the room. Not here. This was her ER, and she was the charge nurse.

Don knew that he would not get far with the 240-pound, five foot four nurse who had a reputation for literally taking down irate patients who came into the ER high on drugs. The most popular story was the one about her subduing a six foot seven, 300-pound man who was high on crack and tried to attack a nurse who wouldn't give him any drugs. They say she came through the double doors from the patient area and hit him with a right. He dropped to the floor, and his black wig went flying across the room. She then sat on him and kept him restrained until the police arrived. Taking that incident into account, Don spoke kindly to Nurse Bell. "Please remind him that I would like to see him."

Nurse Bell smiled, looked at Rod, and said, "Follow me."

Ronnie Parker was in pain from four cracked ribs, a concussion, damage to his pancreas, and internal bleeding.

"Rod," Ronnie's voice was weak. "Be careful tonight. I was on my way to confront Dobie and go to the media when I had an accident. Maybe you should not do the lecture tonight."

"Don't worry, my best friend, my brother in Christ. God is in control. He sent Amy to help me, and I have the word of God on my side."

"Rod, remember that song we learned in church?"

"Which one?"

Ronnie winced as he sang softly. "All night, all day, the angels are watching over me."

"I remember," Rod said.

"Maybe Amy is an angel."

Those were the last words Rod heard his best friend and brother in Christ say. Rod placed his hands over Ronnie's eyes and closed them. He thought about the scripture verse that said, "To be absent from the body is to be present with the Lord."

When he turned around, there was Diane Bell. She had just come back into the room. She walked over, took Ron's pulse, and checked the monitors. "I am sorry for your loss," she said.

With tears falling down his cheeks, Rod declared, "This was not a loss, this was Ronnie's victory. You see, for the saved, to die is to gain. He is now in the presence of Jesus the Christ."

As he walked away, Diane lifted both hands and exclaimed, "Hallelujah! Praise be to God. The man was saved!"

Rod walked back into the waiting room, and Don stood up as he approached. "Oh, no," Don groaned, noting the solemn look on Rod's face.

Rod put an arm on Don's shoulder. "Our friend is with the Lord. There is a chance that you, Dobie, and I might die tonight. I need to know whether you are saved."

"What?" Don was confused.

"Listen, Don. I know what is planned for tonight, but it's not going to happen. As a result, you might be killed. Have you accepted Jesus Christ as your savior?"

"Of course. I am a Christian!" Don said.

"Be very sure." was Rod's earnest reply. "You need to make arrangements for a funeral home to take Ronnie's body. I will see you tonight." With that, he turned and left the hospital.

CHAPTER 32

Police Chief Paul Morris was screaming. His voice was booming from inside his office. He had Detective Smadja, Detective O'Connor, and Officer Lee in his office. From outside of his office, one could only make out a few words like "fool," "crazy," "gun," and "badge." But that was enough to let others know that the live, on-air interview Dobie had done with Sonja Ashby was not appreciated by the chief.

"Detective O'Connor!" the chief screamed. "You have no authority to conduct a press conference without the city manager's and my approval!"

"Chief, I had the city manager's approval."

The chief said, "You are a liar. I spoke with Hart this morning, and he was not aware of the interview, let alone giving you permission."

Dobie's face turned hot red. He had told Don that if he was ever asked if he had given permission for any of Dobie's actions, Don should indicate that he had given authorization.

The chief turned to Officer Lee. "Please tell me how the prisoner escaped."

"I don't know, sir. I went to the lock-up area to check on the prisoners, and she was gone, though the cell was still locked. I don't know. She just disappeared." Officer Lee looked the chief straight in the eye. "She just disappeared!" he repeated.

"Lee, do you think that I am a fool? Do you think I'm crazy?"

"No, sir, but that is the truth."

"Detective Smadja," the chief's voice was calmer. "What was the cause of Craig Newman's death?"

"Chief, Craig Newman, Darryl and Antoinette Poulardi, Carter

Michaels, Alice Parker, Wanda Hall, and Officer Kerry Taylor all died of natural causes—with help."

The chief of police was no longer calm. "Give me your badge and gun!" he roared.

"What?" replied Detective Smadja, thrown off by the chief's outburst.

"Give me your badge and gun. You are obviously unable to conduct an investigation. You have obviously gone crazy."

Detective Smadja pleaded, "Chief, check with Dr. Maxwell. All of the victims looked like they had a stroke, but that type of stroke is not possible. Also, all of their bodily fluids were removed. Dr. Maxwell believes—and so do I—that these are cult killings."

"Hmm," said the chief, walking back to his desk and standing behind his chair. "You and Dr. Maxwell believe we have a cult on our hands. Officer Lee says a prisoner escapes without unlocking the cell door, and with no one seeing her. And Detective O'Connor, you accuse this prisoner of murdering the Poulardis, though at the time she was still sitting in jail. All of you are off this case! O'Connor, you are working the convention center tonight with Officer Lee. Smadja—"

Detective Smadja did not let the chief finish. "I'm off the case too?"

Dobie protested, "Chief, I helped book this event. I know the layout of the center. I should be the one backstage."

"No!" the chief barked. "Now, all of you get out of my office!"

CHAPTER 33

Terri Taylor answered a knock at her brother's front door and was surprised to find Sonja Ashby standing there. "Ms. Ashby," Terri said, "we are not prepared to make any statements."

"I am only here to convey my sympathy to Kerry's wife."

Terri stepped onto the porch and closed the door behind her, causing Sonja to back up a little. "Listen, Sonja. Kerry told me you had a thing for him. You just want to see how the grieving widow is holding up so you can do a report. Well, report this! She is standing on her faith in Christ Jesus. Standing because she didn't lose her husband. She knows exactly where he is."

"And where is that?" the reporter asked.

"With Jesus, Sonja."

As Terri turned around to go back inside, Sonja asked, "Do you have a comment on the fact that Darlene Poulardi is alive and was seen by your brother?"

Terri turned to face Sonja. "No comment."

Sonja waited until Terri was back in her sister-in-law's house before pulling the digital player from the pocket of her waist-length leather jacket. Satisfied that the device had performed well and had recorded her conversation with Terri Taylor, she turned to her cameraman, who had been hiding behind a row of hedges. "Did you get all of that?"

"Don't confuse me with your normal cameraman," Lynn said, "I'm ahead of you. I don't need direction."

Sonja smiled as Lynn got into the WCNE van. "We need to get shots of the people demonstrating, as well as comments from the crowd about the murders. They are already gathering outside of the center. Who knows, maybe death naturally follows Rod Strickland."

* * *

Rod was walking the streets of his hometown, Rachael's Point. He was walking and praying for the city, for tonight's lecture, and for what awaited him at the convention center. He knew that he would come face-to-face with evil tonight. He was sure that he would see Darlene Poulardi in her seventeen-year-old body. He also prayed for the souls of Don Hart and Dobie O'Connor. He prayed that if they had not yet accepted Christ as their Lord and savior, they would do so sooner rather than later.

As he turned onto Franklin Street, Rod was pursued by Mr. Trucelli, a former city council member and now a fretful man with too much time on his hands. Rod remembered that when he was a teenager, Mr. Trucelli had always taken an interest in the youth; though there was no proof, Rod always suspected that the councilman had a thing for Mrs. Parker.

"Rod!" Mr. Trucelli exclaimed while pinching Rod's left cheek with one hand and gently tapping the right cheek with the other. "I am excited about tonight. You know, son, I believe that we have angels encamped around us. I believe that you have a guardian angel, so don't let anyone deter you tonight."

"Thank you, sir." Rod said.

As he continued up Franklin Street, he met three more people who knew him and gave him an encouraging word. When he got to the end of Franklin and was about to turn left onto Roosevelt Street to make a full circle back to Main, where he had parked the GTO, Dobie pulled up beside him in his cruiser and blew the horn.

"Get in!" Dobie called out.

"No, thank you," Rod said, and he kept walking.

"Rod," Dobie said in a less authoritative voice, "get in the vehicle, please. I need to take you over to Haines Street to show you the protesters."

"I've seen the demonstrators in other cities. None of those signs are new to me."

Dobie pulled the cruiser ahead and parked. He got out and walked toward Rod. "Did those signs in other cities accuse you of murdering a seventeen-year-old girl and demand that charges be reinstated?"

Rod stopped walking and turned to face Dobie. "No."

"Listen to me," the detective said. "I am responsible for your safety tonight. I know you can take care of yourself, but I don't know about Ronnie. So instead of Ronnie bringing you to the center, I will pick you up."

Rod was surprised that Don hadn't told Dobie about Ronnie. "I don't need Ronnie to take me. I can drive myself there," he said, thinking it was best to not say anything about Ronnie's untimely passing.

"That's not acceptable, Rod," Dobie said, and he was back to his authoritative voice.

"What are you going to do, Dobie? Put me in protective custody?"

"Strickland, if you get killed or hurt tonight, my hands are clean."

"Dobie."

"What?"

"Killed or hurt by the crowd—or by something else?"

"I don't know what you are talking about."

"Yes, you do, and you think this is going to be a win-win situation for you. You are wrong. You have no idea what type of pact you entered into, and you put the Four under a deathwatch. The only one who is safe now is Ronnie. Dobie, you are an idiot!"

What does that mean? Dobie wondered as he watched Rod walk away. *How much does he know about what was to happen tonight. And how is Ronnie safe?* He would have to get answers to those questions another time, because neither Don nor Ronnie was answering his cell phone.

Rod opened the door of the GTO to find Amy sitting in the front passenger seat. He was not at all alarmed by her presence.

"Amy, I am not sure," Rod began slowly. "Before a lecture, I am normally excited, anxious in a good way, and expectant of what God is going to do for the people in the audience."

"Even for the unbelievers and the protesters?" Amy asked.

"Especially them. They come to protest or disprove what I say, but what happens is that a seed gets planted. But tonight is different. It is not the protesters or those who don't believe. Tonight, I am facing an evil person who wants to kill me."

Amy reached over and clasped Rod's hand between hers. "Rod." She looked him in the eyes. "Don't be afraid. There are more who are for us than against us."

Rod had never before felt hands like Amy's. They were light, and the touch was so soft that if he had not seen her pick up his hands, he would not have known she was holding them. Then as quickly as he had thought about the feel of her hands mingled with his, she released them. Rod was embarrassed and had little beads of sweat on his forehead. He wondered whether Amy could read his mind.

Amy acted as if she did not notice it and said, "This is what I need you to do tonight. Make sure Ronnie has you at the—"

Rod interrupted her. "Ronnie is dead, Amy. He died this afternoon, after being in an automobile accident." The fact that Amy was an angel, and that this was the first time he'd spoken these words to someone who was not an adversary, caused Rod's emotions to burst forth. He began to cry, and then sob and shake. He leaned over the steering wheel and wept.

Amy felt sorry for Rod and rubbed the small of his back. She then managed to lay his head against her shoulder. "Rod, comfort yourself in the absolute truth that he is with Jesus," she said softly. "Let the peace that can only come from God take over your spirit, your soul, and your whole being. God designed us to be able to release emotion, so let it come. I will be right here with you."

CHAPTER 34

Sonja had been with the protestors for over an hour. She had received good insight regarding why they didn't believe in angels. She found a few who knew personal history about Rod Strickland. There was one man, however, who appeared to know so much about Strickland that he could be considered a stalker. Jerry Cummings was a self-proclaimed atheist who'd started following Rod Strickland after he'd heard him lecture in his hometown of Oakland, California. Jerry had first met Rod when he was invited by a friend who'd believed that her mother was now an angel, watching over her and her three children.

In that meeting, Strickland had talked about the Bible. Mr. Cummings had said it was a bogus book. He recalled that Strickland had said, "Angels are encamped around God's people," and Rod had talked about how the heavenly beings ministered to Jesus and spoke with John, Peter, Daniel, and Ezekiel, claiming they were delivered from danger and told of things to come in the future.

"Well," Cummings had asked the angel expert, "where were those angels the night my friend Kansas and her three children were killed by a drunk driver?"

Dissatisfied with the answer he'd received, Cummings, who went on to consume more alcohol than his body could handle, decided that night in Oakland that he would stop at nothing to prove that Strickland was a liar and would cause others to lose their lives. Since then, he had not missed any of Rod's lectures and had shown up at all of his appearances, especially after finding out that Rod had been accused of murdering a seventeen-year-old girl and had not spent a day in jail, but went off to the military, where he was trained and continued to kill.

Sonja asked, "How do you know that?"

"I have my sources, but he was sent on missions to kill teenagers because of his history in Rachael's Point."

"Have you confronted Mr. Strickland with your suspicions?"

"He ignores me and my questions, but I know he murdered those four people here in Rachael's Point. Maybe not physically, but Strickland has an evil spirit."

"I thought you were an atheist," Sonja said.

"I am," Cummings replied, "but I've also seen things at his lectures. Things like protestors suddenly dropping their signs and claiming to accept Jesus as Lord. Strickland does evil things. He plays with people's minds."

Sonja made a few notes and turned to her cameraman. "Let's get into the building and wait to speak with Strickland—or should I say, Spooky Strickland."

"I think you should take Mr. Cummings with you." Lynn said. "A confrontation between this guy and Strickland would make great TV."

Sonja turned. "Mr. Cummings would you like an opportunity to have a one-on-one conversation with Rod Strickland?" Sonja smiled and thought, *This is going to be great.*

CHAPTER 35

Rod was back at the Parkers' house after crying and being comforted by Amy. She had counseled him not to do anything differently from what he was used to doing at his other speaking engagements, and she added that she would meet him at the convention center at 5:45 p.m. Till then, he would read a few verses from the sixth chapter of Ephesians. He would put on the full armor of God as affirmed by the Apostle Paul.

Dobie had just gotten off the phone with Don and was still in shock at the news that Ronnie Parker had died in an automobile accident this morning. He had chastised Don for not calling him immediately, especially when Don had told him there was no need to have called him then because Rod was there. He was sick and tired of Rod, and he would be glad when Darlene finally took care of him. He saw himself going out to the crowd of five thousand to tell them that the presentation had to be cancelled because the speaker had suddenly died backstage of an apparent stroke. He would be sure to look visibly shaken, but his grief would not be for Strickland; it would be for his friend Ronnie Parker.

* * *

It was 4:00 p.m. Dobie was rehearsing the plan to eliminate tonight's keynote speaker.

* * *

Don Hart was growing more scared; He was certain that Rod was aware someone was out to take his life. It bothered Don that Rod seemed not to care that he was in danger. Had Rod made a deal with Darlene, and was the plan now to kill Don instead? He was not about to find out. He would stay away from the convention center and would not be alone tonight in any location. He decided that he would make an unannounced visit to the chief of police and stay with him through the night.

* * *

Sonja was sitting in the news van, going over all of her notes and getting ready for her 5:00 p.m. live feed from Rod Strickland's dressing room at the Rachael's Point Veteran's Memorial Convention Center. She made a note to mention the connection between Strickland, Dobie, Don Hart, and Darlene Poulardi. She also would mention the recent Darlene sighting by the late Officer Kerry Taylor. She smiled to herself. *I am ready for my close-up.*

Amy was in prayer, asking God for strength and guidance. She asked for power and stamina to prevail against the enemy. She prayed for a spirit of fearlessness to overcome the attack of the enemy.

* * *

Detective John Smadja was coming out of the shower, getting ready to pick up the chief coroner, who was as excited as he was about hearing Rod Strickland speak. John had a feeling that with everything that had happened since Mr. Strickland's arrival, tonight there would be more than just a talk about angels. For that reason, he checked his weapon to make sure he had a fully loaded cartridge. He wished that he could pray, but he never felt that he was worthy enough for God to hear his prayers, and he hoped that listening to Rod Strickland would answer some questions. He was hoping for direction that would give him hope for the future. If there were angels watching and protecting humans, he wanted that protection.

* * *

Darlene Poulardi did not care about the time of day. She was at the Benshoff Hill Cemetery, lying prostrate on the floor in Mr. Newman's office, in praise and worship to Angerona. She told the goddess that tonight she would deliver the fluids of one of those who'd tried to humiliate her on that night many years ago, until Angerona had intervened. She would whisper words of mystery and death into Rod Strickland's ear and then collect the fluids, the wonderful nectar for the goddess. She would enjoy bringing about the death of this man who claimed that God was good and that angels encamped around his children. She couldn't wait to see his face and eyes when he realized that there were no angels encamped around him to save him from Angerona and her emissary. She walked out of the building, took a deep breath, and floated upward.

* * *

During this time at the convention center, a large crowd had spilled out of the parking lot, handing out pamphlets and denouncing Rod Strickland and his teachings on angels, God, and Jesus as Lord and savior. Of the five hundred gathered, there were forty to fifty supporters with signs honoring God, lifting up the name of Jesus, and asking the Holy Spirit to touch the heart of those who were blind to the truth of the gospel. The supporters were not from nearby churches. As a matter of fact, there were no churches represented missing the opportunity this would have given as a chance to witness to the lost.

* * *

Rod showered and dressed. He wore his button-down oxford blue shirt, brown khaki pants, blue socks, and brown penny loafer shoes. He put on his navy blazer and walked out of his old bedroom and into Ronnie's. Tears welled in his eyes as he surveyed the sparsely furnished room. "I miss you, friend," he murmured after some time.

When he neared the bottom of the stairs, Rod felt his grief subside and give way to a peace he knew could only come from on high. He descended the remaining stairs with shouts of praise. "Praise God, from whom all blessings flow. Praise him for his son, Jesus the Christ, and for the gift of salvation. Thank you for the angels that you have encamped around me." He got to the door and added, "This night, thank you for the full armor of God."

Unbeknownst to Rod, when he walked out of the Parker house and got into the GTO, he was being watched from both the ground and the air. Dobie O'Connor had been sitting in his 2008 Black Chevy Impala. Darlene Poulardi soared high above the Parker house.

As Rod drove by the screaming protestors, he concluded that none of them had any idea that he was the one they were opposing. He had seen this over and over again, and he had seen the signs before—except for one being held by a young boy of about eight with shoulder-length brown hair, a smooth white face, and green eyes that intently followed the GTO. The boy's eyes almost seemed unnatural. As the car got closer, the boy pointed at the sign that read, "Rod Strickland, you were responsible for the deaths this week in Rachel's Point. Tonight is your night." As Rod passed the green-eyed boy, he saw in the boy's features the eerie, physical manifestation of an evil spirit that dwelled within him. Then the demon spoke through the child host, shouting, "Angerona is waiting! Angerona is waiting!"

Rod began to pray. "Lord, you have not given me the spirit of fear. You have made me more than a conqueror through Christ Jesus. I am equipped with the word of God, and I thank you for the power that you have given me through your word. I claim and stand on your promises. In the name of Jesus, so let it be."

As he drove around to the back of Rachael's Point Convention Center, he saw Amy wearing her black duster. He thought for a second that if she was not an angel, he would love for her to be his wife.

He got out of the car, and Amy asked, "Are you ready?"

"I am."

"I'm not talking about the lecture."

"I know," Rod said. "I just don't know what I'm ready for."

They entered the convention center through the security entrance and exchanged pleasantries with the two guards who were on duty. Rod then went on to oblige the smaller of the two men, who asked for his autograph. After taking a copy of his book from the briefcase he was carrying, Rod signed his name and wrote his signature phrase, "Stay blessed." He finished writing just in time to see Amy smile at him.

Later, as they walked through the corridor behind the other security guard, Amy said to Rod, "Darlene will attack tonight. I believe it will happen before the lecture. Rod, the key is not to allow her to whisper or speak into your ear. If she does, you will die."

They continued down the well-lit corridor and turned left to climb the stairs. At the top of the stairs, they turned right onto tan carpeted floors. The first floor was concrete. They walked halfway down the hall to the elevator, which was on the left. The security guard pushed the up bottom, the elevator doors opened, and the three stepped in. The security guard, who had not spoken a word before, waited until they were safe inside the elevator to ask his question.

"Sir, why do angels exist? God has man to do his work on earth. Why does he still need angels?" This provocative question came from a man who was at least six feet five inches and two hundred pounds of muscle, with dark wavy hair. He appeared to be of Italian descent, and he had a childlike, sincere look about him.

"What's your name?" Rod asked.

"Dino Edwards."

"Dino," Rod began, "this is the short answer. Angels were created to praise God, and to serve and minister to man. I can tell you that if it weren't for angels, many of us would not be here today. I know for a fact I wouldn't be." He looked at Amy and continued. "I also believe that I would not make it through tonight, if it were not for angels."

"How do the angels serve us?" Dino asked.

"Dino, why don't we get together after my presentation? I will go in-depth with you about angels."

A look of surprise came over Dino's face. "You will meet me after your speech?" "Sure," Rod said. "You will be the one escorting me from the arena and keeping the protestors at arm's length, right?"

"Right."

Rod again looked at Amy, "Well, all three of us can eat at Conley's," he declared as they exited the elevator onto the fifth floor.

They stood outside Rod's dressing room. "When you are ready," the security guard said, "I will be right here to escort you to the stage. Mrs. Strickland, I can escort you to the auditorium and have you seated in a secured area."

"No, thank you. I'll be staying with Rod," Amy said hesitantly.

Satisfied, Dino unlocked the door, and Amy and Rod walked in and closed the door behind them.

Upon entering the sitting room, they were shocked at a horrible scene in front of them: two dead bodies, and TV reporter Sonja Ashby curled up in the corner in the fetal position, shaking and crying.

In two long strides, Rod was at her side. "Are you all right?" he asked the frightened reporter.

She looked at Rod with sheer terror and then spoke in between sobs and violent shakes of her body. "She said to … to tell you that she would be back."

Rod and Amy looked at each other. neither had to ask Sonja who she was talking about. Rod took out his cell phone, but Amy grabbed his hand before he could dial. "Who are you calling?"

"The police!" Rod said.

"And what are you going to tell them? Better yet, what will Dobie say when he comes to investigate?"

"What do you suggest we do?"

Amy looked at Sonja. "First, let's find out what happened."

Rod had already helped Sonja to the couch. She had curled up on one end tightly, as though trying to make herself invisible. Amy walked over to her and slowly knelt in front of her. "Sonja," she said. There was no response, no movement other than her eyes going from left to right; then she would look up at the ceiling.

Amy used a little more authority, "Sonja, what happened here?"

The woman did not respond. Only the movement of her eyes showed that she was alert. Without warning, Rod sat down beside Sonja and slapped her across the face.

"Rod!" Amy said in astonishment.

"I'm sorry, Sonja, but we need to know how these people died."

Sonja put her hand on the spot where Rod hit her. "We were here to interview you and watch Jerry Cummings confront you."

"Who is Jerry Cummings? Amy asked.

"One of the demonstrators."

"How did you get past security?" continued Amy.

"We had a police security pass from Detective O'Connor."

Rod's patience was again running thin. "Why did you want—"

"It doesn't matter, Rod!" Amy interrupted.

Rod glared at Amy. "It matters to me."

Turning her attention back to Sonja, Amy asked, "What happened after you came into the room?"

"This teenage girl was in here. I thought she might be a groupie. She smiled at us and said hello. She then walked over to Mr. Cummings, gave him a hug, and whispered something in his ear. Just like that, he fell to the floor. The girl then looked at my cameraman with what seemed like the eyes of a demon. They were blazing with lust, but the lust for death.

"She started for Lynn, who had captured Jerry Cummings on camera swooning to the floor. When he pointed the camera at the young woman, she struck one of several poses before taking the camera from Lynn and setting it on the floor. After she whispered in Lynn's ear and he too collapsed, I started screaming. I ran for the door, and she grabbed me and threw me into the corner. She then came floating toward me."

"She what?" Rod wasn't sure he'd heard her right.

"She floated toward me." Sonja repeated, now sitting up straight but still not moving much. "I thought she was going to kill me. She pointed to me and said to tell you that she would be back." Sonja hesitated before saying anymore. "That strange girl told me to tell Rod Strickland that Darlene Poulardi would be back."

Amy turned to Rod and said, "We need to get Dino out of here."

"No!" Rod said. "We need to get him *in* here. Darlene is on a killing spree, and I don't want another death." Without waiting for a response, Rod opened the door.

"Is everything all right, Mr. Strickland?" asked the security guard.

"I need you to come inside, please."

"Yes, sir."

CHAPTER 36

Dobie pulled up to the arena. *God, I hate protestors. I wish we could shoot them all.*

"Detective O'Connor! Detective O'Connor!" Dobie turned to see Detective Smadja and the coroner. He nodded his acknowledgement and continued on. He didn't get very far before the coroner caught up with him and asked, "Any more murders to report?"

"Not yet, Bernie," Dobie said dismissively.

"Are you on your way up to Strickland's dressing room? If so, I would like to join you."

"Yes, and no," Dobie snapped. "Yes, I am on my way to Strickland's dressing room. No, you can't come with me. Detective Smadja, please come and get your friend!"

Dobie walked away with long strides, making sure the diminutive coroner could not keep up with him. At the center's front entrance, where most of the police officers were stationed for crowd control, he checked with each officer; all reported that there had been no incidents. He checked with Officer Monroe Reese, an officer who was very ambitious and who recognized that a promotion was dependent on his contacts in the department. Who better to be connected with than Detective Donald O'Connor Jr.? "Officer Reese, any problems letting in the reporter?"

"No, sir. She and her entourage, a camera man and another reporter."

"I told you the reporter, not the entire news team."

"Sorry, Detective."

Dobie pushed past Officer Reese, heading toward the elevator that would take him to the fifth floor and to Rod Strickland's dressing room. He decided to take the stairs instead, not wanting to get there before or while Darlene was engaged in her work.

CHAPTER 37

"What the ...?" Dino couldn't believe his eyes. In the two years that he had been a security guard, he had never had to fire his gun. The closest he had come to witnessing a death was when a concertgoer ran over a cat that lived in the woods behind the arena. Now here he was, standing in a room with two dead bodies. "We need to call the police!" he said, reaching for his radio.

"Wait!" Rod shouted. "This may be the work of someone in the police department."

Confused, Dino waited for Rod to explain. Before anyone else could speak, however, the door to the suite opened and then closed.

"Dino, Rod! Get behind me! Rod, get Sonja off the couch!" Amy yelled frantically.

She moved to the center of the room for a better view of the entry way. Clearly, she was the only one able to see whatever or whoever had entered the suite.

Though still confused at the dramatic scene unfolding before him, Dino got in line behind Rod, who had reached over to take Sonja's hand. The distraught woman had become more agitated and had dug herself deeper into the sofa, all the while repeating, "She's back! She's back!"

Rod felt sorry for the woman. Following Amy's order, he picked her up and placed her in the corner, where she'd been when they'd first entered the suite. He motioned to Dino to stay with her.

A huge surprise awaited him when he returned to the sitting room where he had left Amy. There was his high school friend Darlene Poulardi. A seventeen-year-old Darlene Poulardi not walking or flying, but gliding into the suite from the hallway. Her blonde hair flowed down and over her black duster. She had on a black silk blouse, black jeans, and black boots. Rod almost chuckled at the sight of the stunningly beautiful girl floating on air, but the seriousness of the moment made him think better of it. This was not magic. Darlene was there to kill him, take his body fluids, and offer them as a sacrifice to the goddess Angerona. It was 6:32 p.m.

* * *

At the same time Darlene Poulardi was squaring off with Rod and Amy, Pastor Franklin Kimble was in Dallas, Texas, with his prayer team as they prepared to take phone calls from viewers of those who would be watching the taped broadcast of last Sunday's sermon. This was a normal pre-broadcast meeting, but at 6:32 p.m., two minutes after they had gathered, Pastor Kimble fell to his knees and asked those who were with him to do the same. He then led them in prayer for the safety of Rod Strickland.

* * *

Amy looked at Rod and said, "I thought I told you to get into the other room."

"Hello, Rod. It's been a long time," Darlene said cheerily while lowering herself to the floor. "This won't take long. I just need to tell you a secret."

Amy moved toward the evil enchantress and said with authority, "In the name of "Jes—"

"Don't speak that name in my presence!" Darlene yelled.

"Jesus!" Amy finished. "Your mission and your evil plans will not prevail. Darlene Poulardi, tonight you will die for good!"

Darlene sprung and struck Amy with the back of her hand. Not only did blood spurt from Amy's lip, but the blow knocked her onto the floor. "I am going to kill you just for fun of it, after I speak with my friend Rod," Darlene said.

Rod looked at the blood coming from the left corner of Amy's lip. *Angels don't bleed*, he thought before turning his attention back to

Darlene. Her eyes were clear, but she had no spark of life in them, only a cold, deep void. This frightened him.

"Rod," Darlene began as she lowered herself back to the floor, "I always liked you. You were not like Dobie. It's a shame that you got mixed up in the plan to embarrass me. It's a shame that you weren't man enough to say no. It's a shame that Wanda, my mother and father, Detective Taylor, and Mrs. Parker died because of you. It's a shame that you are not going to live to see your next birthday." Those were Darlene's last words, before Dino struck her with the full force of a blindside tackle, which seemed to take the breath out of her.

Rod almost felt guilty at seeing Darlene collapse under the impact of the riveting punch to her jaw, but when she rebounded and grabbed Dino's head, pulling him to her, Rod lunged after Darlene in an effort to save the security guard from certain death. He was too late. Darlene succeeded in whispering into Dino's ear, and her newest victim lay dead on the floor.

Rod became enraged. "What did you do?" he screamed.

Darlene ignored him and pulled out a vial to collect the dead man's body fluids.

Amy, who had gotten back up on her feet, looked from Rod to Darlene. "You are a tool of Satan, Darlene. Don't let him use you to kill."

"I am not killing. I am the purifier, and I am the balance sheet."

"You are a pawn for Angerona, a demon directed by Satan."

"She's not a demon—she is a goddess who gives life."

Rod was adamant. "Angerona promotes death, not life. How many have you killed for her?"

"Why does she need the fluids?" asked Amy.

Darlene stopped her advance toward Rod and turned to Amy. "The same reason your God needs blood. For eternal life for those who believe in her."

"Darlene," Amy replied calmly, "the blood that God requires for eternal life has already been shed. That was the blood of Jesus—shed once at the Cross of Calvary for the salvation of the whole world."

Darlene placed the vial of fluid in the holster inside of her duster. "I have one question, Amy. Is this salvation available to me? Will it allow me to keep my youth and my beauty?"

"No," Rod answered.

"I didn't think so." With that, she pounced on the angel lecturer, knocking him to the ground. On the way down, Rod struck his head on the corner of the oak table that was in the middle of the suite and was knocked unconscious. Darlene whispered in his ear, but nothing happened. She swore under her breath, knowing that an unconscious victim who was unable to hear her whisper would not succumb to death.

Determined to get that second vial of fluids, Darlene turned and faced off with Amy, who was ready for battle with Darlene. In her hands were two gold-tipped steel stakes that were sharpened by powers beyond this earth. She carried them in the special lining of her duster and had removed them just before Rod fell unconscious.

Facing Darlene, Amy spoke loudly and vehemently. "In the name of the one who rules the land and the sea, and every living creature in the air, on this earth and under the earth. By the power of the mighty true and living God, who has given me authority over you." Upon uttering those words, Amy plunged the stakes into Darlene's heart.

Darlene grimaced, drew in a deep and long breath, and then laughed raucously. "You can't hurt me," she taunted. "I am the daughter of Angerona!"

But whatever supernatural powers she had were short-lived. No sooner than she spoke those mocking words that Darlene doubled over and clutched her stomach. A yellow fluid began pouring from the wound in her heart, and vapor rose from her gaping mouth. Suddenly she started to age, her body swelling and stretching as her seventeen-year-old physique gave way to the more mature form of a woman in her early forties.

Amy watched in amazement at the metamorphosis of Darlene Poulardi. "You were wrong," she told the girl. "God is sovereign."

As though Amy's words were bullets from a pistol, Darlene staggered, fell backward, and died instantly.

Amy stepped over Darlene's body and went over to check whether Rod had a pulse. "He will be all right," she said to herself. She turned to

Sonja and motioned for the reporter to come to her. Sonja got up slowly and joined Amy at Rod's side.

"Listen, Sonja," Amy began. "Rod is going to be all right. I have to leave, but I need you to call the police and tell them what happened here."

Sonja was in a daze, staring at Rod.

"Sonja, look at me," said Amy. "Do you understand?"

"I'm listening." Sonja said, her voice barely above a whisper.

"Make sure that you tell the whole story, so that everyone in Rachael's Point will know that Rod Strickland is a man of standard and virtue. Make sure they know that demons exist, as do angels."

"I will," Sonja replied, this time looking Amy in the eye. "Are you an angel?"

"No. I'm a protector."

Seconds after Amy left the room, Rod began to rouse. "What happened?" he asked Sonja.

"You need to ask Amy."

"Where is she?"

"I'm not sure. She didn't say where she was going."

"Sonja, call the police and ask for Chief Morris or Detective Smadja. Whatever you do, do not let Dobie O'Connor into this room."

"Where are you going?" Sonja asked nervously.

"I am late for my lecture."

"Rod, I ..."

Rod placed his hands on Sonja's shoulders. "You can do this," he said. "You are Sonja Ashby, reporter for WCNE." He handed her his cell phone and said, "I want this back."

She smiled weakly. "I'll give it back later—at your exclusive interview with me."

They both smiled, and Rod left the suite as Sonja was saying, "911? This is an emergency."

Rod started to take the elevator, but changed his mind. As he neared the stairwell and opened the door, Dobie caught a glimpse of him as he reached the 3rd floor landing. Dobie was suddenly afraid. *Something must have gone wrong.* Strickland was supposed to be dead by now. Darlene was supposed to have killed him.

Dobie realized that he needed to be somewhere safe. He quickly made his way to the third-floor elevator, The door opened immediately. Once he got to the lobby, he would go to his father's house until he knew what had happened in Strickland's suite.

Detective Smadja and the chief corner had just sat down in the Magnolia Room at the

convention center when his cell phone rang. "Detective Smadja," he answered. It was Police Chief Morris telling him there had been another murder and asking him if he knew where to find Detective Dobie O'Connor.

"Come with me," Detective Smadja said to the coroner. "There has been another murder."

"What? Where?"

* * *

At 7:00 p.m. the announcer walked out on the stage. "Ladies and gentleman, welcome to Rachael's Point Veteran's Memorial Convention Center for a night of revelation."

Detective Smadja stood in the aisle, waiting to see if the event was going to be cancelled because of the death of the keynote speaker. But apparently the presenter knew nothing of the kind, because he continued to praise Rod's accomplishments to the delight of the eager crowd. It was only after he had called for Rod twice that the man became uncomfortable. He kept looking off stage and then back at the audience. Detective Smadja said to no one in particular, "Oh, my God. Not him."

Just when it looked like the announcer was going to have to entertain the audience to keep the agitated crowd from losing faith, there came a thunderous applause as Rod Strickland emerged from the left side of the stage. Rod apologized to the silver-headed man, who quickly handed him the mic and told him, "I'm just glad you're here." Rod faced the crowd, bowed humbly, and began his address the same way he had been doing since his first lecture. "Thank you. To God be the glory. Give him the praise!"

It made the detective's heart glad to see Strickland alive. For a moment, he had wondered if the angel expert had also fallen prey to the entity responsible for the recent murders in Rachael's Point. Relieved, he left the auditorium and was now on his way to find Sonja Ashby, the TV reporter who'd called the station just now, saying she was at the scene of a triple homicide that had occurred in Rod Strickland's suite. Behind him, he heard Rod say, "This has been an extraordinary day for me. I have encountered a demon and either an angel or an extraordinarily godly woman. Before we start, let's pray." It was 7:05 p.m.

CHAPTER 38

At 7:05 p.m., a lone figure was standing on the highest point of Benshoff Hill. Her hands were stretched toward the heavens, tears streamed from her eyes, and her duster blew in the wind. "I praise you, Father, for the strength you have given me to overcome the demons that were sent to destroy. Thank you for the protection you afforded to Rod Strickland. Thank you my God for my assignment, and for the weapons of warfare. Thank you for the truth of your word. Thank you for your son, Jesus the Christ, for salvation." With that, she fell to her knees and wept.

EPILOGUE

Forty-eight hours later, Greg Holmes, the top news anchor for WNNS, started his 7:00 p.m. news program with an announcement. "Good evening, ladies and gentlemen. Welcome to a special broadcast. Do angels exist? Are there demons that roam the earth, killing and robbing people of their lives and even their very souls? Until I met with my guest reporter, Sonja Ashby, I would have said no. However, last week in a small town in Pennsylvania, called Rachael's Point, things occurred that make me rethink my belief." Greg turned to Sonja. "Welcome."

"Thank you, Greg," replied Sonja. She then looked into the camera and thought to herself, *Here I am on WNNS, with my biggest story ever.*

Her station manager back at WCNE was very instrumental in getting her the hour-long news special. He told her that this would put her, the station, and the town into the headlines. Sonja wanted to get this right not for the station, the town, or herself, but for Amy, who'd saved her life.

She looked into camera one and began her story. "It all started with a group of teenage boys who called themselves the Four. Twenty-four years ago, the night of the senior prom, one of the boys convinced the other three to humiliate the most popular and most hated girl in their high school, Darlene Poulardi."

At the Rachael's Point airport, no one was paying attention to the WNNS news broadcast until the familiar face of local reporter, Sonja Ashby, came on the screen. Rod, who was checking his boarding pass, was joined by Amy, and they both looked up at the television.

"Some week," said Rod. "Now Rachael's Point will be a hotbed of reporters for the next few weeks."

"More important," Amy said, "the demonic movement of Angerona will be exposed for what it is."

Rod added, "Thanks to Sonja and her team at WNNS, people will also know that God has equipped certain persons to take on and defeat evil spirits."

The voice on the airport intercom interrupted their conversation. "We are now boarding flight 532 for Denver, Colorado."

"Let's go, Rod," Amy said, picking up her bag.

"What?" Rod said. "I am on the flight to Dallas."

Amy smiled and handed him a boarding pass. "Your plans were changed."

"How did you …? And when did you do this?"

"It was taken care of for us."

"By who?"

Amy simply smiled.

"Hey," Rod said, "you said you were not an angel."

"I'm not."

"Who are you, then?"

"For now, your companion on the flight to Denver and your friend. Are you coming?"

Rod grabbed his carry-on. "I believe, madam, that you are being directed by God. Where he leads me, I will follow."

Rod looked up at the television screen one last time as he and Amy got in line behind the other passengers waiting to board the plane. There was a picture of Detective Dobie O'Connor Jr. with the caption: "Wanted for conspiracy to commit murder."

Rod shook his head and handed the attendant his boarding pass. The young lady, who had red shoulder-length hair; green eyes; a round, cute face; and perfect teeth said, "God bless you and Amy, Mr. Strickland, on your next battle in Denver."

The End

ABOUT THE AUTHOR

Richard I. King is the creator of three television shows, a former teacher, and a mentor to pastors and ministers across the country. Known as a motivator, creative thinker, and man of faith, he loves to share the beauty of God in the world. He has been married for twenty-five years and is blessed with two wonderful daughters.

CPSIA information can be obtained
at www.ICGtesting.com
Printed in the USA
FSOW01n1433110118
43326FS